# Good Ol' Boys

A few years ago I met one of the boys—by then a man, of course—I had formerly worked as a bellhop with. He was the owner of an automobile agency in a large southwestern city, and I also was enjoying some small success. Naturally, we fell to discussing the other boys we had known, those whose later lives were familiar to us.

One had been killed by the FBI while resisting arrest as a suspected kidnapper. One had been hopelessly crippled while attempting to blow up a safe. Two had committed suicide when still very young men. One had overdosed himself with salvarsan, bit his tongue off in a spasm of agony and drowned in his own blood.

## Also by Jim Thompson

### NOVELS

Now and On Earth • Heed the Thunder
Nothing More Than Murder
Cropper's Cabin • The Killer Inside Me
The Alcoholics • The Kill-Off* • The Criminal
Recoil • Savage Night • A Swell-Looking Babe
The Ripoff** • The Golden Gizmo**
A Hell of a Woman • The Nothing Man*
Roughneck** • After Dark, My Sweet
Wild Town • The Getaway • The Transgressors
The Grifters • Pop. 1280 • Texas by the Tail
Ironside (novelization of TV series) • South of Heaven
The Undefeated (novelization of screenplay)
Nothing But a Man (novelization of screenplay)
Child of Rage • King Blood

**\*Published by**
**THE MYSTERIOUS PRESS**     **\*\****forthcoming***

# BAD BOY

## JIM THOMPSON

**THE MYSTERIOUS PRESS**

New York • London • Tokyo

MYSTERIOUS PRESS EDITION

This Mysterious Press Edition is published by arrangement with
Donald I. Fine, Inc., 128 East 36th Street, New York, N.Y. 10016

Cover design by Irving Freeman
Cover illustration by Stephen Peringer

Mysterious Press books are published in association with
Warner Books, Inc.
666 Fifth Avenue
New York, N.Y. 10103
A Warner Communications Company

Printed in the United States of America

First Mysterious Press Printing: July, 1988

10  9  8  7  6  5  4  3  2  1

# I

M Y EARLIEST RECOLLECTIONS are of being pinched. Not in the figurative sense, but actually. I was an awkward, large-headed tot, much prone to stuttering and stumbling over my own feet. My sister Maxine, though somewhat my junior, was quick-moving, quick-thinking, glib and extremely agile. When my actions and appearance irritated her—and they seemed to almost constantly—she pinched me. When I failed to respond quickly enough to her commands, she pinched me. The metaphor, "as smooth as a baby's skin," has always been meaningless to me. My infant hide appeared to have been stippled with a set of coal tongs.

One day, shortly after the Thompson family fortunes had undergone an unusually terrifying nosedive and we had moved into a particularly execrable section of Oklahoma City, Maxine spotted two Negro children returning home from the grocery. They had a large bottle of milk with them.

1

Bringing me up from the steps with a quick pinch, Maxine dragged me out to the sidewalk and accosted the two youngsters.

Would they like to be white? she inquired. Well, in return for their milk, she would perform the transfiguration. She had done the trick for me, and I had been blacker than they were. Much, much blacker . . . and now just look at me.

The tots were a little dubious, but, being pinched, I loudly swore to Maxine's tale. And, being pinched again, I hurried into the kitchen and got the implements—a bar of soap and a scrubbing brush—with which the transformation was to be effected. At Maxine's instigation, I took the patients out to the back-yard water hydrant, and began scrubbing them. Maxine took their milk into the privy (it was that kind of neighborhood), drank all she could hold, then dropped the bottle down the hole.

Emerging, she entered the house, beginning to scream with horror as soon as she had got through the door. Mom came running out, Maxine in the vanguard. Pretending to pull me away from the puzzled Negroes, she got in several energetic pinches, making me howlingly incoherent by the time Mom reached the scene. She gave the tots the price of a fresh quart of milk, wiped them off and dragged me into the house, declaring that she didn't know what she was going to do with me. Snickering hideously, Maxine remained in the yard, free to go about her devilish designs.

Being very young, I was unable to explain the affair within the time that it would have done any good to explain. I got an impression from it, however, very nebulous, then, but one that expanded and jelled later.

I was going to catch hell no matter what I did. I might as well try to enjoy myself.

# II

I WAS ALWAYS a sucker for friendship. Anyone who spoke a friendly word to me could have the Buster Brown blouse which I customarily wore. In my earlier years, my father traveled considerably about Oklahoma, seldom staying in any town more than a month—not long enough for me to become accustomed to a strange school, yet too long for me to lay out. Just about the time I began to get acquainted, we would pull up stakes.

So I hungered for friendliness, and no matter how many times I was duped I never ceased to bite on the bait that was put in front of me. There was a game called "push-over" in those days. A boy would come up to you, put his arm around your shoulder and engage you in kindly conversation. Then, just when you were beginning to warm up to him, another boy would kneel behind you, the first would give you a push, and you would fall backwards on your head.

I don't know how many times I fell for this game, and similar ones, before I began to get the idea that what appeared to be friendship might be something else entirely. I never liked the idea, and I fought against it. In later life, more or less as a duty, I would draw back from a proffered kindliness and coldly demand the reason for it.

In time, my father settled more or less permanently in Oklahoma City where he became the law partner of Logan Billingsley, brother of Sherman, the Stork Club proprietor. In the early days of Oklahoma, Pop had been a peace officer, and had saved Logan from being lynched. I know nothing about the merits of the case, but I do know that they became close friends and later partners.

Logan had a son named Glenn, a more mischievous brat than which never lived. I understand that he is now running a swank restaurant in Hollywood, but that has nothing to do with this story.

Glenn led a charmed life. One Saturday afternoon when he was leaning out the office window, he fell out. But he survived the four-story fall with no more than a scratch. He landed on the awning of the street-level drug store, went on through it, and dropped into a baby carriage. The vehicle was empty of its occupant, fortunately, for he made a wreck of it. But, as I say, he wasn't hurt a bit.

We lived over in the west end of town, in the vicinity of the Willard school, and a very tough section it was in those days. I came home nightly with large chunks missing from my person and attire. Glenn came in always whole and happy, and usually bearing a quantity of valuables which had had other owners that morning.

One morning a bunch of older boys dropped him down a manhole and sealed the lid back on. Most lads in such a situation would have perished of fright, but not Glenn. He wandered around through the various arteries of the sewer, picking up a sizeable quantity of small change from the silt along his way. After a few profitable hours of this, he made his way out through another manhole. He then phoned the police, quoting that a friend of his had been thrown into a sewer by a certain group of boys—he gave their names. Then, without giving his own name, he hung up and went into town.

The cops collared the youths at school and readily wrung a confession from them. The victim was identified as Glenn. A search of the sewer was begun for his body and the young criminals were taken to the police station, facing a long stretch in the reformatory.

Late in the afternoon, Glenn put in his appearance and was hailed by the admiring and relieved police as a hero. They brought him home where he was tucked into bed, apparently too shocked by his experience to eat. Actually, there was nothing wrong with him but a stomach-ache and, perhaps, eye strain. He had visited four picture shows and eaten several dollars' worth of candy, ice cream and other delicacies.

After that experience the worst toughs at school shied away from Glenn. He was pure poison.

I always admired him.

# III

LOGAN MOVED ON to New York and greener pastures, and Pop became associated with another attorney, Tom Connors. Tom had been quite a famous man, and he still was a topnotch lawyer when he was sober. He was a good shot and never without a pair of ivory-handled forty-fives given him by the bandit, Pancho Villa.

With two children and another on the way, Pop was becoming a little worried about the future. So, as a backlog against the uncertainties of the law business, he bought a small neighborhood grocery store in the east side of Oklahoma City. He was out of town much of the time, so it was up to Mom and us kids to look after the store.

There was a large garden in the back yard, and also a pear orchard. Our living quarters were in the rear of the store. With free rent and free vegetables and fruit and a small steady business, it looked like we had the financial problem licked.

In this, we figured without Tom Connors.

He came out from the office one summer afternoon when Pop was away, drinking but not in bad shape. We gave him the spare bedroom and left him alone. After a brief nap he went out the back door and came back with a couple of quarts of booze. Then he began to prowl around the back yard.

We had finished eating by the time he returned, and he had finished the bottle, and there was an expression of deepest consternation upon his face.

"My dear Mrs. Thompson," he said, in his best courtroom manner, "what means have you taken to protect that very valuable pear harvest? Do you have a night watchman or a watch dog?"

"No." Mom smiled hesitantly.

Tom shook his head grimly.

He was, he said, my father's friend. As such, he did not propose to see him stripped of his chattels without a protest. He would take care of the pear orchard himself. When Pop returned there would not be so much as a single pear missing.

Procuring a ball of wrapping twine from the store, he went into the back yard and climbed up a tree. He laced the twine back and forth through the twigs and branches, forming a sort of giant cobweb among them before he fell to the ground on his back. Nothing daunted, he climbed into another tree and treated it as he had the first. And so on to the next, and the next.

There were twenty trees in the orchard. I think Tom must have strung well over a mile of string through them. Then, with the cooperation of Maxine and me, he filled a number of tin cans with pebbles, placed a few cans in each room of the house, and tied the end of a string to each of them.

Well, there weren't any pear thieves around that night (although we could never convince Tom of the fact), but there was a high wind. The trees began to sway and dip. The pebble-filled cans started leaping. A barrage of rocks whistled through the rooms, smashing windows, light fixtures and china. Tin cans crawled in and out of the beds. Wrapping cord—miles of it, seemingly—sought grimly to truss us up.

Struck and snagged in some very tender spots, I started squawking for Mom. Maxine miraculously found me in the dark and pinched me. Mom tried to smack both of us and almost broke her wrist on the bed rail. Then, Tom waked up.

He leaped to the floor, a forty-five in each hand, and cried out that we were being raided. Shouting wild instructions in Mexican, he sprang for the back door. Immediately his feet were entangled in a score of cords, and his flailing arms were likewise caught and made helpless. He struggled onward manfully, dragging the cans with him, along with debris, bedclothes and lighter bits of furniture. At last, however, he stumbled, struck his head against the door-casing with the sound of a bursting pumpkin, and fell down.

He began to snore peacefully.

Mom lit a candle, and came in and looked at him. Her face was pretty grim. She was swinging a catsup bottle in one hand. Finally, after an obvious struggle between her better nature and her natural impulses, she threw a blanket over him and we all went back to bed.

Tom got up ahead of us in the morning to go after more whiskey, and by the time we arose he was anything but contrite. Fortified with several stiff slugs, he led us out into the back yard and commanded us to look upon the wreckage there. Would we now tell him (he asked) pointing at the fruit-littered ground, that thieves had not been out during the night. He denied that there had been any wind.

With Mom protesting angrily, Tom went around and posted himself at the front door of the store. Fingering his forty-fives, he questioned and harangued and threatened every patron who sought to enter. He called them by fearful "aliases" and recited their "records" to them. Some of them fled, and some, of sterner stuff, merely stamped away in high dudgeon.

Around noon a tall heavy-set man bearing a briefcase turned in at the walk: Pop. He got Tom to go to bed and, later, to a "cure." A week or so after that we disposed of the store.

In that time, as I remember, we didn't have a single customer.

# IV

POP WAS PRACTICALLY self-educated, his financial position was more often than not insecure, and he was careless about dress and the social niceties. But few men had as many friends among the great, the would-be and the near. Few men had their advice so sought after.

Pop had a horror of ignorance—I'll tell you why, shortly —and had made himself an expert on almost everything. Politicians, from presidents to ward heelers, prized his opinion on political matters. Grain speculators consulted him on the crop outlook. Wire services quoted his predictions on the outcome of prize fights and horse races. He knew more about law, accounting, agriculture and a dozen other professions and pursuits than many men who made them their life work.

In the early twenties when we were living in Fort Worth, Texas, Dr. Frederick A. Cook, the Polar explorer, was our dinner guest one night. Doc had entered the oil business a short time before and was riding high. He was renting three floors of a downtown office building, he employed close to a thousand people, and his postage bill alone ran twenty-five hundred dollars a week.

He had brought a batch of advertising literature out for Pop to look at. Pop did.

"Don't send this out, Doc," he advised. "It'll put you in the pen."

"Aw, now, Jim," Doc laughed, annoyed. "My copy-writers have worked on that for weeks. I've got thousands of dollars tied up in printing. What's wrong with it?"

"It violates the blue-sky laws. Your attorneys can show you where."

"But my attorneys say it's all right!"

Pop shrugged and changed the subject. Or tried to. Cook insisted on arguing about the literature. He finally got a little angry about it.

"The trouble with you, Jim," he declared, "is that you're afraid every club is going to fly up and hit you. You're wrong about this deal and I'll prove it to you. I'm going into the mail with this stuff tomorrow!"

He got a twelve-year stretch in Leavenworth.

Pop was a wizard in large affairs, but in mundane matters he was a flop. You couldn't convince him of the latter. Periodically, he went on family-management sprees, and he either refused to admit the horriferous results or attributed them to our failure to cooperate.

As an eight-year-old, I can remember his asking Mom about my tastes in literature. He expressed his dissatisfaction with her reply by going out and buying a twelve-volume set of American history and another set of the letters of the presidents. And he pooh-poohed her angry opinion that the stuff was too old for me.

"You're bringing these children up in ignorance," he declared. "Now, when I was four years old, I could name all the presidents and . . ."

There followed a long list of accomplishments, of which I was no more capable than I was of flying. (I suppose the comparison shamed me all my life.) But for months afterward, I was required to read the books aloud to him every night. I read them at home, while at school I read the adventures of Bow-wow and Mew-mew, and Tom and Jane at grandmother's farm.

In the same fashion, I was drilled in higher accountancy before I had mastered long division; I was coached in political science before I ever saw a civics class; I learned the dimensions of Betelgeuse before I knew my own hat size. I was always a puzzle and a plague to my teachers. I often knew things that they didn't but seldom anything that I should.

I don't mean to give the impression that Pop was harsh. He was anything but. He seldom raised his voice. Never once did he so much as paddle one of us kids. It was simply that he couldn't be content to manage his own sphere and let Mom manage hers.

Every once in a while he would get the notion that we weren't eating properly, and he would undertake to "put a little meat on our bones." These undertakings usually manifested themselves as great messes of what he called "succotash"—beans, tomatoes, corn, peas, and perhaps a bottle of catsup, all cooked together in the largest kettle he could find. Mom would sternly forbid us to eat any of it, so Pop, after disposing of a quart or two, would take the receptacle under his arm and go around and make gifts of it to the neighbors.

It was Pop's greatest fault that he could seldom see bad in anyone. He did not want it pointed out to him, and he refused to admit it when it was. After we sold our grocery store, we moved over on West Main Street in Oklahoma

City. There was a family across the street whose little girl was always fighting with Maxine (or vice versa) and Mom, after a few words with her mother, decided that they were trash. Pop said that she shouldn't make statements of that kind. We weren't really acquainted with the people and shouldn't form judgments until we were.

Pop had served us "succotash" that evening, and Mom was not in the best of humor.

"If you think so much of them," she suggested, sweetly, "why don't you call on them? Take them some of that stuff. They look to me like they'd eat anything."

There were a few more words, and, finally, Pop got up and put on his hat. Taking the kettle under his arm, he marched stiffly out of the house and across the street.

Some thirty minutes later he returned—and with him he brought the detested neighbors: the man and woman and their little girl. The man was a small wiry fellow, with the bluest eyes I have ever seen. The woman was a gaudy, gushy type. At Pop's instigation, they were paying us a social call.

Mom sat with her lips compressed, emitting monosyllables when she was forced to. Pop, of course, became more and more hospitable.

It developed that the man was the local agent for a St. Louis automobile dealer, and Pop promptly announced that he was interested in buying a car. Before the visit was over he made an appointment for a demonstration.

When our visitors had finally departed Mom began to laugh rather wildly.

"You buy a car! Are you crazy, Jim Thompson? We've got another baby coming, and we owe everyone in the country now. And you talk about buying a car! I'll just bet you that fellow is a criminal! I'll bet he steals those fine cars he drives around!"

Pop said this was preposterous. "I refuse to discuss the matter further."

"Well, you won't catch me riding with you! Me or any of the kids . . ." And we didn't go, either.

So Pop went for the ride alone, and several others. The price of the car was surprisingly cheap—so much so that Pop, who was usually agile in such situations, found it difficult to avoid buying, and Mom, who loved a bargain, wavered somewhat. But having stated so often that the man was a criminal, she would not back down.

It was just as well. I cannot remember the guy's last name now, although I should, as many crime stories as I have written. But his spry mannerisms and his bright blue eyes had earned him the sobriquet, among the police of six states, of "Monkey Joe." He was the southwestern outlet for a gang of Missouri car thieves who had hundreds of thefts, and, I believe, thirteen murders to their credit.

At the time the pinch was made Freddie, my other sister, had just been born, and we had other things than crime to talk about. But the magazine sections of the Sunday papers kept the case alive until we were less preoccupied. For weeks they were filled with the pictures and exploits of "Joe, the man with the monkey-blue eyes"—which may or may not explain why there was a sudden dearth of Sunday papers around our house.

Pop said there was no connection.

# V

ONE DAY AROUND the turn of the century, a large young man with the profile of President McKinley wandered into Territorial Oklahoma from Illinois. He had a certain ponderosity of manner which set none too well with his background. For, while he could be considered unusually well-read for his day, he had little formal education, and his working experience was confined to a few months as a railroad fireman and a year or so as a country schoolteacher.

He conferred with a highly placed Republican relative— Territorial Oklahoma was governed by Republicans—and this man got him an appointment as a deputy United States marshal. He did not ask for help after that, nor did he need it. For the young man's chief talent was something he had been born with, the ability to make friends. And, I may as well say now, it was to prove no unmixed blessing.

When statehood came, he ran for sheriff in a solidly Democratic county and won by a landslide. He was re-elected for two successive terms, and, except for larger plans, could have held the office indefinitely. The ultimate objective of those plans was the presidency of the United States—for the man believed, and did until the day he died, that any man could be president. As a long step toward that goal, he won the Republican nomination for Congress from his district.

Here, at last, the man's talent for friendship became a curse. A man's best friends, once they turn upon him, become his worst enemies. It was so in the young man's—I may as well say—my father's case.

Pop's honesty was something painful to behold. In the relatively minor office of sheriff, he had seen no occasion to discuss his early history and antecedents, nor to promulgate any but the most general of platforms. As a congressman, however, he felt that his constituents had a right to know all about him and what to expect of him as a legislator. Though it damned near killed him—and I mean that literally—he told them.

The great body of voters—men who had moved into Oklahoma from the deep south, men who had told each other fondly that "Ol' Jim ain't like the rest of them No'thuhnuhs" —heard him in shocked silence, then with purple-faced fury. They learned that the S in his middle name stood for Sherman, after General Sherman with whom his father had marched to the sea. They learned that the South, whether it liked it or not, was part of the United States, and the quicker it accepted the fact the better. They were told that, as a Republican, he stood for the absolute equality of all races, and that he would fight to obtain and maintain that equality.

Needless to say, Pop's honesty cost him the most smashing political defeat in Oklahoma history.

Not only that, but it also made him a fugitive from justice for more than two years.

Like many other frontier peace officers, Pop had been decidedly careless in his official bookkeeping. He knew very little about such work, and he was too busy, or so he thought, running down outlaws. He knew that neither he nor his deputies had ever pocketed a penny of public funds. That being the case, what did it matter if, at the end of his third term, his books showed a technical shortage of some $30,000.

As a matter of fact, it wouldn't have mattered at all except for the debacle of his congressional campaign. Everyone knew he was honest. No one was going to make even an implied assault on a man with thousands of voters in his pocket. He planned, as soon as he had the time and money, to hire a corps of expert accountants and get the sheriff's office mess straightened out. But the end of the congressional race found him without money, virtually without friends, and with an overwhelming host of enemies who intended to see that he was given no time to adjust his accounts.

Overnight, he was faced with criminal charges and the almost certain prospect of a long stretch in prison. Knowing of nothing else to do, he fled to Mexico.

What had been an unusually promising career was now, obviously, at an end. Since he could barely support himself, he was to all purposes permanently estranged from his wife and two small children. He had no money and no way of earning any except by competing on even terms with peon labor. Rather, I should say, uneven terms. The Mexican government had no love for Americans who took jobs from its own starving nationals.

I don't know what other men would have done under such circumstances, but I can speak for myself: I'd have walked into the Rio Grande and kept on walking until my hat floated.

That wasn't, of course, Pop's way of doing things.

All man's troubles, he decided, sprang from ignorance—

in this particular case ignorance of law and accounting. He did not know enough, but he would henceforth. He would acquire the knowledge to solve this immediate difficulty, then go on to improve and expand his learning in every possible field.

Somehow, he managed to acquire the funds necessary for correspondence courses in law and accounting. During every minute he had free from drudgery, he studied. After some two years, he received an LL.B. degree by mail, as well as a certificate as an expert accountant. Meanwhile, he had got in touch with former intimates in Oklahoma. Feeling toward him had died down. If he wanted to come back, they'd stake him to expenses and also go his bond while he was fighting the case.

Pop went back. He audited his own accounts and then argued his own case in court. He proved that not only did he owe the county nothing but that the county actually owed him several thousand dollars.

Eventually, he became attorney and official accountant for the Oklahoma Peace Officers Association and developed a large private practice. But even when he was well on the road to success, his open-handedness and his reluctance to dun a client brought on long periods of financial destitution. During such times, Mom, Maxine and I resumed a practice we had begun when he fled to Mexico.

We went to live with Mom's folks in a Nebraska country town.

# VI

COULD SAY a great deal about the unpleasant features of living with relatives, of living in a gossipy small town where everyone knows your circumstances and has little else to talk about. But I have brooded overlong about these matters in other books (and out of them); so let us dismiss them with the statement that they did exist. Along with everything else, I often managed to have a wonderfully amusing time.

For this, for the attitude which enabled me to have it, I am largely indebted to my Grandfather Myers, the most profane, acid-tongued, harsh, kind, delightful man I ever knew.

I recall an evening when my ultra-pious grandmother had dragged me to a country revival meeting, and I lay shivering in my dark bedroom afterwards. I was too terrified to sleep. I was certain that my six-odd years of life—all spent in sinning from the preacher's standpoint—had earned me one of the hotter spots in hell, and that I would certainly be snatched there before morning.

Then, though I had made no sound—I knew damned well what my grandmother would do if I waked her up—my grandfather crept in in his undershirt and trousers. "Can't sleep, huh?" he jeered, in a harsh, mocking whisper. "Let some goddam fool scare the pee out of you, huh? Well, goddam, if you ain't a fine one!"

He ordered me into my overalls and led me out of the house, pausing in the kitchen where he picked up a pint cup of whiskey toddy which he always kept warming on the back of the stove. We went out into the back yard and sat down on the boardwalk to the privy. There, after each of us had had a mighty sip of toddy and I had been allowed a few puffs from his Pittsburgh stogie, he delivered himself of a lecture.

I cannot repeat it here, his acidly profane yet somehow hilarious discourse on certain types of religionists and the insanity of taking them seriously. Suffice it to say that, coupled with the toddy, it sent me into muffled gales of giggles. It sent me smiling to sleep, and left me smiling in the morning.

Having suffered the cruelest of childhoods himself, my grandfather believed that anything that contributed to a child's peace of mind was good, and that anything that disturbed that peace was bad. I hold to that same belief. It is one of the very few things I do believe.

Grandfather, or "Pa" as he was known to the entire clan, was an old man from my earliest recollection—just how old even he did not know. Orphaned shortly after birth in a period of indifferent vital statistics, he had been handed around from one family to another, worked always, fed seldom, and beaten frequently. For all that his memory could tell him he had been born big, raw-boned and doing a man's work.

He might have been fifteen when he enlisted as a drummer boy in the Union Army, but he believed he was nearer ten. By the end of the war he was a full-fledged sergeant, an inveterate gambler, a confirmed drinker, and a stout apostle of the philosophy of easy-come easy-go. He didn't know what he wanted to do, but he was certain that it must pay a great deal and have very little physical work attached to it.

There was no such vocation, of course, for a brash young man who could barely read and write. Back in his home state of Iowa, he worked for a few years as a stone mason, the only trade he knew, and usually gambled away his money as fast as he got it. When his luck at last changed for the better, he took the resulting several hundreds and went to St. Louis. There he sat in one of the big games for seventy-two hours straight, leaving at its end with more than ten thousand dollars.

He liked big things, simply for the sake of bigness, and about the intrinsically biggest business in those days, for the small capitalist, was hardware and farm implements. Pa bought out his hometown dealer in those things and set out, to all appearances, on the career of a prosperous and respectable merchant.

These appearances were deceptive. He was not respectable, by many definitions of the term, and any prosperity he may have enjoyed was as brief as it was accidental. He liked to gamble and carouse as much as he ever had. He felt a fatal friendliness for the financially distressed, and as fatal an indifference for the well-heeled. To his way of thinking, the loss of one's money in a poker game was an entirely valid reason for failing to pay a bill, and to such an unfortunate he was prepared to extend credit indefinitely. Fiscally excellent risks, on the other hand, were apt to be dunned ahead of time and to have their bills padded: this on the theory that they had probably stolen their money, anyway, and that he could put it to better use than they could.

But his biggest trouble, perhaps, was his complete unreaddiness to settle down. Now "chained," as he thought of it, to a wife, children and business, he grew more impatient with every passing day. He could not bear to haggle. A customer who hesitated over a purchase would first receive a sharp reduction in price, and then, if he still hesitated, the exasperated suggestion that he get the hell out until he made up his mind.

Such shenanigans as these could only end in one way. Very late one summer's night, Pa loaded a covered wagon with his family and such personal chattels as he could get onto it and quietly drove away, leaving his home and his business behind him. The word "his" is used loosely. They were no longer his and the lighter articles he carted away would not have been if his creditors had caught him.

He homesteaded in Nebraska territory, and, for more years than he cared to remember, he did two men's work. He farmed, he ran a dairy, he carried on an extensive masonry contracting business. Finally, as he was nearing the age of fifty, he paused to take inventory.

He owned his own comfortable home and several acres on the edge of town. (And he had set his married son up on a valuable farm.) He owned several small rental properties in the town proper. It was enough, Pa decided. With his Civil War pension, he could get by nicely. For the rest of his life, he would never do another damned lick of work.

He bumped his masonry carts together, loaded them with tools and implements, piled his working clothes on top— and set fire to the lot. Then, donning his "gentleman's" uniform of blue serge suit, large black hat, and Congress gaiters, he set about catching up with his fun.

Alas, times had changed sharply for the worse during his long spell of industry. There were no *real* gambling games any more—only penny-ante skirmishes which were an insult to a spirited man. There were no real two-fisted drinkers any more—only molly-coddles who sipped half-heartedly at their drinks and then went on about their business. There were no *real* men any more. If you "called" a man, the ninny would have you hauled into court instead of making the proper response with fists and feet.

A practical man (by his own admission), Pa drew such satisfaction as he could from his whiskey jug, his boxes of long black stogies, and verbal jousting with his wife. But the first two were only adjuncts to the good life, not the life itself, and my grandmother would not play fairly with him. After a few relatively feeble remarks about how "nasty-mouthed," "filthy," and "no-account" he was, she would simply lock herself in her room, leaving Pa more frustrated than ever.

Surcease came—or, rather, began—with Pa's decision that he needed a horse and buggy to get around in. There are tamer animals in the jungles of Africa than the one he brought home. Not only was it unbroken, as the seller had honestly pointed out, but it declined to be broken. And, slowly, as the terrifying beast kicked to pieces his brand new buggy, Pa's face lit up in a beautiful smile.

That was the beginning. The end did not come until Pa, by breeding and selection, had populated the barnyard with the muliest cow, the fightingest chickens and the fiercest hogs ever assembled by man. The chickens did not lay and were too tough to eat. The hogs were lean, muscle-bound warriors which no stock-buyer would have as a gift. The horse could not be made to perform for more than a few minutes at a time. The cow—the only one I have ever seen do so—gave skimmed milk and very little of that.

Pa loved them all. They gave him what he needed.

Every trip into the barnyard was an adventure. The chickens ran at him, wings beating furiously. The cow butted and tried to crush him against her stall. The hogs were constantly attempting, with occasional success, to knock him down and gnaw on him. The horse kicked, bucked and nipped.

The animals were at some disadvantage in being unable to curse, but otherwise the incessant warfare was carried on on terms as even as Pa could devise. The kicking horse got kicked. The butting cow got butted. The zooming chickens, with their furiously beating wings, were in turn zoomed at, Pa thrashing his arms wildly. The hogs, who used everything they had on him, got considerably better than an even break. Pa met their onslaughts with nothing more than his boots and cane.

Although Pa's bathing was confined to washrag-and-basin dabbling, this should not be interpreted as meaning that he was hygienically careless. He simply had his own ideas about personal hygiene. Nights, mornings, and numerous times in between, he took great draughts of whiskey to "kill the poisons" in his system. To maintain his body at the same even temperature, he wore heavy woolen underwear winter and summer. He ate large quantities of liver, brains and kidneys (to fortify his own). And bedtime found him battening down every window in the house to shut out the noxious night air. Finally, to get back to the subject of animals, he would not sit down in the privy in the normal fashion, but stood up on the seat and hunkered over the hole.

He was in this semi-helpless position one day when the privy door blew open. A huge dominecker rooster, seeing a once-in-a-lifetime chance, dashed in and pecked him severely about the loins. Pa was outraged by this grossly unfair attack, but he did not resort to an axe as a less fair man would have. He simply ignored that particular rooster from then on.

When the fowl flew at him, he would ward it off brusquely or merely step aside, then calmly proceed on his way. After a few days of such rebuffs, the rooster began to stand by himself in lonely corners of the barnyard. His comb wilted; his beak drooped nearer and nearer to the ground. Now and then the other chickens, always quick to spot an outcast, would swoop at him and peck him sharply on the head. But he never fought back.

One day, when he was dreaming no doubt of happier times, he wandered too close to the hog lot. A sow poked her snout through the rails and ended his misery forever. Pa said it served the son-of-a-bitch right, and let that be a lesson to me—why me, I don't know—but I could see that he was badly upset over the affair. Stamping into the house, he emptied the pint toddy cup without pausing. When my grandmother, anticipating the usual outburst of prandial profanity, remarked that if he didn't like her cooking he knew what he could do, Pa only looked at her moodily. In fact he ate almost a half a pie—"leather and lard," to use his customary appellation—before getting back to normal and hurling the plate into the garden.

All my life I have been the victim of the inhumane and unjust botching of potentially good food. My mother was a woman of indifferent appetite, and thus lacked the basic essential of a good cook. My wife—well, my wife is a wonderful cook, but I usually do the family cooking. I got ptomaine poisoning from the very first restaurant meal I remember eating. Looking back from my present state of antiquity, I can't recall eating more than a few dozen good meals that I did not prepare myself.

If I dine at a friend's house a treasured recipe, handed down in the family for generations, will suddenly go sour. A restaurant with an unimpeachable reputation will blithely risk all for the dubious pleasure, say, of serving me stale eggs fried in goat grease. I have known but one other person to suffer from such a frightful conspiracy. A small con man named Allie Ivers (of whom much more later), he had a way of protesting which only insufficient nerve has kept me from using.

Allie owned an enormous sponge, selected with much care for its unusual powers of absorption. Before dining out

he would fill this sponge with dirty water. When his meal
was served him, he would slide this sponge under his napkin, hold the napkin to his mouth, and . . . but need I say
more? Suffice it to say that the sight of Allie staggering
about in apparent agony, a horrible liquid spouting from his
napkin, could empty a crowded restaurant in the space of
five minutes.

But I was about to speak of Ma's—my grandmother's
cooking. And since I cannot use Pa's descriptive terms, and
no others are adequate, I am somewhat at a loss as to how to
proceed. I must settle, I suppose, for the statement that nowhere—in hobo jungles, soup kitchens, greasy spoons,
labor camps—nowhere, I repeat, have I eaten anything as
bad.

The good woman was an omnivorous reader of farm-
magazine food and health "authorities," and her ideas
changed with theirs from day to day. Salt caused hardening
of the arteries—so that condiment might be omitted from a
dish which had to have it. Baking powder "had been known
to cause digestive disturbances"—so Ma, until she was advised to the contrary, would leave it out of her biscuits. On
the other hand, a few drops of vanilla added to baked beans
not only gave them an "unusually piquant" flavor but was "a
certain safeguard" against pellagra. So you know what went
into the bean pot.

It made no difference to Ma that one might prefer un-
piqued flavors, pellagra and even death to beans with vanilla
in them. You got vanilla. At least you got it until she
learned, say, that leftover chocolate custard made a "marvelous addition"—whatever that meant—to Boston's favorite
vegetable.

The fact that Ma might not have any leftover chocolate
custard was no deterrent to her compounding of such a recipe. She would make some and leave it over. Ma, need I say,
had a decidedly literal mind.

Mom, Maxine and I were in no position to complain, although, following Pa's precepts, I often did to my eventual sorrow. But Pa protested enough for all of us. Insofar as he could, he stuck to a diet of meat, cooked by himself or eaten raw, and he encouraged us to do the same. But every mealtime brought on an outburst of profanity, table pounding and hurled dishes, as furious as it was futile. It was one of my regular after-meal chores to go out into the garden and bring in any dishes which had not been shattered.

I think the fates must have provided Ma with a steel-lined stomach as recompense for depriving her of all sense of taste. In no other way can I account for her ability to eat heartily and healthfully of her own fortunately inimitable cooking. As for the Thompsons, I think we certainly should have died except for Pa's constant dosing of us with whiskey.

Both on arising and retiring, we were required to take generous drinks of toddy. And when school was in session, we kids got another big drink upon our arrival home in the evenings. In winter, the whiskey was a cold preventative, to Pa's notion; in warm weather, it served to "purify the blood." In days to come, I was to regret this early acquired taste for alcohol. But, at the time, I do not believe we could have survived without it.

While Ma could botch a meal quite capably by herself, it cannot be denied that she received considerable inadvertent assistance from Pa. For Pa was the official firebuilder, and he pursued this vocation more as an outlet for his tempestuous temperament than for any utilitarian purpose.

Pa began the chore by opening all the drafts on the kitchen range, and walloping it fore and after with an extra-heavy duty steel poker. This shook the soot out of it, so he said (and judging by the ineradicable carbon-hue of the kitchen there was no reason to doubt him). It also put him in the fine and furious fettle necessary for the task ahead.

Removing every lid from the top of the stove, Pa piled in kindling, corn cobs, coal, newspapers and everything else handy with a wild indiscrimination that was marvelous to behold. Onto this pile, which normally extended a foot or so above the top of the stove, he dropped an incendiarist's handful of burning matches. Then, snatching up a gallon can of kerosene, he emptied the better part of its contents into and over the range.

No fire in the hell which Pa incessantly referred Ma to could have been more awe-inspiring. It didn't just burn; it exploded. It groaned and panted and heaved, snatching at persons and objects ten feet away and leaping clear to the ceiling. By the time it had burned down enough for Pa to replace the stove lids, weird things were happening to its internal structure. Coal was smothering the kindling; half-burned newspapers were clogging the drafts. According to whim, it might go out entirely at the very moment Ma began her alleged cooking. Or, suddenly puffing smoke and sparks through every crevice in the range, it might begin to burn anew and with an intensity that made mock of the original blaze.

Beyond beating it with the poker, which he was ever ready to do, Pa refused to take any responsibility for the stove's fractious actions. It wasn't his fault if Ma didn't know how to keep a good fire going. Anyway, as he pointed out with some truth, nothing short of taking Ma out and shooting her—a course he frequently recommended—could greatly improve the household cookery.

# VII

VERY EARLY ONE morning Pa poked me into wakefulness with his cane and presented the inevitable cup of toddy. I was to get dressed and come quietly out of the house at once. He was going to take me to see what "a bunch of god-damned fools look like."

I obeyed, of course, and as we strode away from the house in the dusky dawn, his calloused hand gripping my small one, Pa jogged my memory with a little jovial profanity.

No revival meeting was complete in those days without a prediction from the preacher as to the date when the world would end. The preacher who had scared the daylights out of me had stated that six calendar weeks from the day of his departure the world would be no more.

Very few of the townspeople had taken this nonsense literally—not sufficiently so, at any rate, to act upon it. But, silently, Pa had marked those few well, and shortly we were standing before the residence of such a family.

Pa, who had known almost exactly what to expect, emitted an amazed and scornful snort, and loudly proclaimed that he would be goddamned. What, he demanded of me, as though I were personally responsible for the sight, were this man and his wife and their three children doing in their nightgowns? And why had they climbed upon the roof of their modest cottage? . . . Well, (having partially answered his own questions) why the nightgowns? Were they going to spend all their time in heaven sleeping? And why stand on the roof? Didn't they think God could lift 'em all the way? Didn't they know He could spot as big damned fools as they were even if they hid in the cellar?

This indirect quizzing of the pious porch-perchers was just getting under way when, from opposite directions of the street, two furious clouds of dust appeared. They came parallel with us simultaneously, and from them there eventually emerged Pa's son and son-in-law, respectively my uncles Newt and Bob. The two men joined us on the walk, and where Pa had left off in his razzing they took up.

When the possibilities of the situation were exhausted, all of us hurried on foot around the town, "before the damned fools (could) come to their senses." But I think I shall drop the curtain on that tour. While I tried to outdo my relatives in laughter that morning, I actually felt a strong sympathy for those we laughed at. I winced for them—and I still do. Perhaps because I have been a bigger fool so many times myself.

Newt—we did not use titles such as "uncle" and "aunt" on my mother's side of the family—was a better-educated version of his father without, however, possessing quite so much of Pa's rough good humor. He had been farming on his own for only a few years when he came off second-best in a battle with a horse, and his left foot had to be amputated. And, possibly because he tried to walk without a crutch or cane (no one was going to make *him* a cripple!), the stump became infected.

Periodically, thereafter, he had to be operated on. He had to submit to the gradual trimming away of his leg and the fitting of a succession of artificial limbs. He was in almost constant pain, and his surgical expenses were enormous. Yet, as he went about the tilling of a large farm and the rearing of a big family, he never complained. There was a surly undertone to his laughter—but he did laugh—and he was apt to be painfully sardonic and sarcastic even in kindness—but he was kind.

An Englishman of noble family, my Uncle Bob had settled in this small Nebraska town for reasons he never revealed. He began his business career there as a storekeeper, branched from that into dealing in land, and wound up as a banker. Although not a modest man in many ways, he took no credit for his success but attributed it all to the invention of the cash register. Except for that splendid device, he could not have trusted his affairs to employees, thus leaving himself free for increasingly larger and profitable ventures.

Bob had an ironclad rule never to touch his capital for living expenses. He also insisted on making an annual and substantial increase in that capital. He was the local agent for dozens of items, ranging from patent flea-soap to gasoline lamps, and persons who borrowed money from him were apt to find themselves loaded with these things as a condition for receiving their loans.

Most practitioners of the sharp deal are close-mouthed. Not so, my Uncle Bob. To anyone he could buttonhole, he bragged about how he had "stung" this person or "skinned" that one.

Actually, as I came to learn in time, Bob's avariciousness was a pose. His schemes and his jeers were simply his way of making small-town life bearable. Like Pa, Bob was far too big a man for his environment. The only way he could endure it was to dwell in a kind of tantrum. Secretly, Bob was one of the most generous men in town.

Although we must have been aware of each other before then, I seem to have made almost no impression on him, nor he on me, until I was almost seven. The occasion was dinner at his house. He was seated at the head of the long table, and I at the foot, and in between were his wife, his six children, his four Persian cats and his two Airedale dogs. There was a long hickory ferrule at his side which he wielded throughout the meal, occasionally correcting a cat or a dog with it, but, more frequently, smacking his children when they erred in etiquette. Betwixt ferocious scowls at me he sent his off-spring to the front room, by turns, to rewind the phonograph and replace one classical record with another.

I was greatly awed. When, abruptly, he asked me if I knew what Brann's *Iconoclast* was, I could scarcely gather my wits sufficiently to stammer out an affirmative.

"Something to eat, isn't it?" He beamed at me falsely. "Something like cornflakes."

"N-no," I said faintly. "It's a magazine."

Bob chortled sarcastically, wagging his head in ironic wonder. A magazine, eh? Oh, that was very good! I would tell him next—he supposed—that Shakespeare was not the name of a fountain pen! I would tell him that, would I? And he bared his teeth in so terrible a grimace that my hair literally stood on end.

Nevertheless, I told him, even as he had prophesied.

Bob snarled at me hideously, then suddenly threw out another question. "Who," he said, "was Scoopchisel?"

"S-scoop . . . ? I don't know," I said.

"You—don't—know? You don't know!" His face colored in a spasm of rage and bewilderment, and, for a moment, I thought surely that this was to be my end. But somehow, though the effort was obviously a drain in his innermost resources, Bob managed to bring himself under control. He addressed me at length and with patience, a fond glow coming into his fine gray eyes. And always thereafter, I discovered, I could move him into this benign mood by raising the subject of Scoopchisel. Scoopchisel, the greatest writer of all time, a man robbed of his proper due by his sneaky brother-in-law, Byron.

It was Scoopchisel who had written the immortal lines:

> So get the golden shekels while you're young
> And getting's good.
> And when you're old and feeble
> You won't be chopping wood.

But he was at his best when annotating the work of other poets. To Fitzgerald's inquiry, "I often wonder what the vintner buys, one half so precious as the stuff he sells," Scoopchisel had retorted, "Protection!" Anent Pope's statement, "Hope springs eternal in the human breast," Scoopchisel had said, "Until you're married, then it moves its nest."

I was so impressed with the works of Scoopchisel that even after Pop and the rest of us had reassembled and I was well advanced in grammar school, I quoted him. Which inevitably led, of course, to my inditing a pained and accusing letter to my Uncle Bob. He replied promptly.

He would not advise me—he wrote—to accuse my teachers of ignorance, nor would he confess that Scoopchisel had never existed. He would only say that every man had to believe in something and that he liked to believe in Scoopchisel, and even though the latter had never lived he damned well should have. "In short," Bob concluded, "keep your hat on and your head ducked. The woodpeckers are after you."

Newt and Bob had sons approximately the same age and some eight or ten years older than I was. Two more inventive, mischievous lads would be hard to find, and they stood always ready to supply any devilment which I could not dream up for myself. One of our more successful enterprises was the electrification of certain privy seats around the town. My cousins did the wiring, and supplied the dry cells. I, lying with them in a nearby weedpatch, was allowed to throw the switch at the crucial moment. There are no statistics, I suppose, on the speed with which people leave outdoor johns. But I am certain that if there were, the victims of our rural electrification project would still be holding the record.

I entered the first grade of school in this town, and shortly thereafter I had reason to complain to my two cousins that my teacher was picking on me. The good youths were seriously disturbed—or seemed to be. We retired to the loft of Newt's barn to confer. There, after we had all had a good chew of tobacco and a swig from a purloined bottle of wine, they reached a decision.

My teacher, they advised me, was suffering from a malady known as horniness. She "wanted some but didn't know how to get it." It was their suggestion that I linger in the schoolroom after the class had gone out and jab her "where she lived." This would show her that I was a "pretty gay guy" and my troubles would be well on the way toward their solution.

Well, I had seen just enough of the mating antics of farm animals to accept this scheme as entirely plausible. I became so enthusiastic, in fact, that my cousins began to believe in the stunt. They fell for their own rib as hard as I had. Excitedly—and no longer joking—they repeated their instructions, adding a message for me to pass on to the teacher. I was to tell her that they were rarin' to go, any time and place she suggested, that they would undertake to do their best for her and she would leave the trysting place relaxed and rejoicing.

That was not the exact message, but it conveys the general idea. The words my cousins used, while considerably more graphic, were somewhat less polite.

So I trotted off for school the next morning, silently rehearsing the scene I was about to play—convinced that happier days were just ahead. True to my instructions, I lingered behind at recess time. When I at last started out the door where the teacher was waiting impatiently, I triggered my forefinger and jabbed. Then, having proved I was a "gay guy," I started to deliver my cousins' message.

I didn't get as much as a word of it out before the teacher, an apple-cheeked German girl, affixed her hand to my ear and hauled me squawling toward the principal's office.

I was saved from I don't know what unpleasantness by two circumstances. First, the teacher's sense of delicacy prevented her from more than hinting at the nature of my crime. The strongest indictment that the principal could evince from her was the statement that I had been "pranking nasty." Secondly, this principal, like many another person in the town, was in the financial clutches of my Uncle Bob and was reluctant to offend him—as he felt he would—by punishing me.

So he gave me a mild talking-to, after the teacher had been sent on her way, plus a pat on the head and the suggestion that I pattern my conduct, in the future, after "that splendid uncle of yours." Then, I was dismissed to the playgrounds. I looked up my two cousins, forthwith, and charged them with giving me some very bad advice. They, having lost much of their previous day's enthusiasm, were vastly relieved to learn that I had not involved them, and they readily acquiesced to my demand that I give each a "swift kick in the arse." Thus, the matter ended.

Whether my teacher was any kinder to me thereafter, I don't remember—probably she had been kind enough in the first place. I do recall that never again did she come within my reach. She was no fool, even if I was.

These cousins of mine operated under a peculiar code of logic which, although it seemed entirely clear and sensible to them, was as maddening as it was incomprehensible to the outside world. Even I, a sympathetic participant in most of their stunts, was baffled and bewildered by them more often than not.

One spring, when the boys had foresworn crime for several months—and there was a growing feeling that they might escape death by hanging, ending their existence with nothing worse, perhaps, than life imprisonment—their delighted families presented each with a handsome bicycle. I was on hand at Newt's farm where the presentation ceremonies were held, and an impressive occasion it was.

As head of the clan, Pa spoke first, punctuating his blood-curdling remarks with wild slashes of his cane which might well have brained less agile youths. Newt and Bob were the next speakers, in that order, brandishing their respective cane and ferrule. Then, with the air sizzling with profane threats, the ladies stepped forth wielding whips and switches. And while their vocabularies were free of curses, their lectures were nonetheless fearsome and awe-inspiring. The general feeling seemed to have been expressed by Pa's declaration that the boys had better, by God, behave themselves and take care of their bikes or they would be nailed to the barn door and skinned alive.

The boys listened with seeming meekness. Then, accompanied by me, they repaired to the interior of the barn where they proceeded to disassemble the bicycles into several hundred odd pieces.

Discovered in this outrage, as they soon were, the two youths pleaded for time. Given a matter of a week, they promised, and they would convert those childish playthings, the bicycles, into a thing of great beauty and utility. Exasperated and exhausted, the adult relatives gave their consent without striking a blow.

The week passed in a hubbub of furious activity. The boys acquired several sheets of stout roofing tin. They got hold of a quantity of hard wood and steel rod and paint, and the basic parts of an old gasoline water pump. Assisted by me, they pounded and sawed, shaped and soldered, painted and sawed and bolted together. And by the eve of the seventh day, so very real—though often misdirected—was their genius, they had created an automobile.

It looked like an automobile—save for the wheels—down to the minutest detail. It ran quite as well as many of the automobiles of that day.

Our adult kin were both dumbfounded and delighted as we made a brief trial run up and down the barn corridor. All unsuspecting of the ultimate and abysmal objectives of the two youths, they made no protest when the latter announced that the first full-scale demonstration would be held on the morrow.

Both my cousins and I spent the night at Newt's house. The following morning, attired in our Sunday's best, we marched haughtily into the barn. We tuned and oiled the motor of our automobile until it purred like a cat. We wiped the gleaming red body free of the last speck of dust. Then, we climbed into the front seat, with me in the middle, and drove grandly out into the yard.

We circled it twice, allowing our beaming relatives and the neighbors they had pridefully summoned to feast their eyes upon us. With this, the promised demonstration taken care of, we suddenly roared full-speed to our previously determined destination—the open door to the food cellar.

The door was flush with the ground and opened into a long steep flight of stairs leading under the house. We went crashing and smashing down them, shedding fenders and other of the automobile's components as well as sizeable bits of our own epidermis. Then, at the bottom, where the steps ended in an upright door, the engine shot from beneath the hood and we shot over it. The whole house shook with the impact of flying bodies and machinery, and the explosions of fruit and vegetable jars.

Bruised, bleeding and besmeared, we managed to claw our way back to daylight and the fearsome reception awaiting us. But the automobile had so wrecked the stairs and jammed into the lower door that no one could get back down into the cellar.

As soon as he could do anything but curse, Newt announced that he was through. "I give up, by God," he stated, and he declared that since the family was cut off from its supply of fruit and vegetables, they could all simply die of scurvy and the sooner the better. "There's a hell of a lot worse ways of dying," he pointed out grimly, and no one could gainsay him.

Fortunately, after a few weeks of meat and gravy and the like, and when scurvy seemed actually imminent, he was persuaded to adopt a more sensible course. The result was a new entrance to the cellar through the kitchen floor, a new door and new stairs—and complete physical exhaustion for my cousins and me. For Newt, naturally, did not lift a finger on the job. He was one of the three foremen—Pa and Bob being the other two. And so well did they handle their duties, we were hardly able to stir from our beds for a week.

The one last piece of orneriness which my cousins and I collaborated in almost got us all killed. It came about after much reading and discussion of the literature of parachuting, an art then in its infancy.

Mom and we kids were preparing to rejoin Pop in Oklahoma, and the various connections of the family had gathered at Newt's house for a farewell Sunday dinner. When the meal was over, my cousins and I slipped out to the barn loft where, earlier, we had concealed three bed sheets and a

length of clothesline rope. In no time at all we had para-
chutes—I don't know what else to call them—tied to our
shoulders, and were ascending the sixty-foot tower of the
cow lot windmill.

It was a cold, windy fall day. Shivering, I looked at the
stock tank adjacent to the mill, studied the four-foot depth of
water which was supposed to "break" our fall. Shivering, a
little sick at my stomach, I wanted to withdraw. But my
colleagues jeered me hideously. At one and the same time,
they swore that I was a damned cowardly calf and a mighty
brave kiddo. So up the tower I went.

My cousins followed me, goosing and punching one another. Arrived at the top, they ordered me to move around
the platform to make room for them. I tried to, but the platform was small. The only way I could hang on was by
reaching up and grasping the direction-arm of the windmill
fan.

The action coincided with a sudden, sharp gust of wind,
and this, with my weight, resulted in disengaging the lock-
ing device. Before I knew what was happening, the mill had
begun to spin and *I* was swung out into space, jerked and
flung first one way then another.

My cousins ducked and cursed frantically as my flailing
feet almost knocked them from their perch. Shouting at me
to "drop in the tank, dammit," they both tried to scramble
down the ladder at the same time. Neither would give way to
the other, and they jammed there, tangled in a mass of sheets
and clothesline. I continued to swing this way and that,
screaming, my eyes clenched tightly.

The back door of the house opened and people streamed
out.

Pa, Newt and Bob were in the vanguard—the first two
waving their canes, Bob brandishing a long hickory ferrule
which he was seldom without and usually found use for.
Behind this trio came one of my aunts, carrying a buggy

whip, another equipped with a piece of harness strap, and Mom and Ma armed with switches, a plentiful supply of which was always kept around the house.

They might not know how to get us down from the tower, as soon became apparent. But they had plans for us, obviously, when we did get down. All my mother's family were like that, and yet they were warmhearted, children-loving people, too. It was simply second nature with them to attack every situation with acid words on their lips and a weapon in their hands.

Gathered around the base of the tower, around the tank, they shouted up incoherent directions and threats. Mom tried to climb up after me and was dragged back. Pa and Newt gave the wooden uprights a severe caning.

Above the turmoil there suddenly came the sound of splintering wood, and the step to which my cousins were clinging gave way. They went plummeting down into the tank, landing squarely on their backs. The water rose out of the vessel and descended upon the waiting posse. The latter, cursing and screaming according to sex, latched on to the two youths and proceeded, as the saying was, to tan their hides.

This exercise, coupled with the cold water, so calmed my relatives that they at last thought to relatch the lock on the mill. I was able to swing back to the platform, and thence descend to earth where, everything considered, I got off pretty lightly since everyone was exhausted.

# VIII

M Y SISTER FREDDIE was born during a severe economic depression. It was a hard winter for the nation in general and for the Thompsons in particular. Pop had begun to dabble in the oil business, and not very profitably. Mom was in the hospital much of the time.

Our house had twelve rooms (Pop had felt that we needed something larger with the advent of Freddie), and the fires of hell couldn't have kept it warm. The plumbing was constantly freezing and bursting. I froze and burst out with cold sores which my schoolmates promptly diagnosed as cancer. Looking back, I find my cold sores to have been the one cheerful facet of that winter. I had but to wave my festered hands and the toughest bully in school fled before me shrieking.

There were repercussions with my recovery, but even these worked out to my advantage. I got a great deal of splendid exercise in racing up alleys and shinnying over back fences. My reflexes became trigger quick. Without losing the look and the feel of it, much of my awkwardness disappeared.

To take Mom's place while she was in the hospital Pop hired a woman who, with undeserved generosity, shall be known herein as Mrs. Cole. A large puffy woman with a ragged topknot of walnut-stained hair, she was the indigent relative of some friend of a friend of Pop. That was all the recommendation he needed.

I came home from school one night and found her lying on the lounge in the front room. She was wearing house slippers and a shapeless mother-hubbard. She waved at me limply and remained prone.

"Let's see, now," she said. "You're Johnnie, ain't you?"

"Huh-uh. I'm Jimmie."

"You hadn't ought to say huh-uh, Johnnie. You ought to say yes ma'am and no ma'am."

"Why?" I said.

Mrs. Cole frowned slightly but made no answer. She intended, apparently, to make friends with me. "I got awful bad rheumatism, Johnnie. I can't do much. You're sure going to help me a lot, ain't you?"

I said I guessed I was. "What you want done?"

"Help me set up, Johnnie."

I took her by the hands and helped her to sit erect. Groaning and panting prodigiously, she got to her feet. With a kind of funny feeling in my throat, I watched her go into Mom's room and close the door.

After a few minutes she came out, smelling strongly of medicine or something, moving much more spryly. Maxine came in and was put through the same rigmarole that I had been. At first Maxine said no, she wasn't going to be a good girl and help a lot. Then she said maybe she would.

"What time does your pappy come home?" Mrs. Cole inquired. And learning that he was due any minute, she went into the kitchen. When Pop arrived she was setting the table, obviously suppressing great pain.

Pop was impressed and alarmed. "You'd better sit down awhile," he suggested. "There's no hurry about supper."

"Oh, no," said Mrs. Cole in a piteous voice.

"But you're sick. Do you want me to get a doctor?"

Mrs. Cole said she was past the point of being aided by doctors. "I'll be all right, Mr. Thompson. I been sufferin' for twenty years and I reckon I can stand a few more. Don't you worry none. I ain't going to be no burden on you."

"Why, of course you won't be," Pop declared warmly. "You just sit down, now, and I'll fix things. Jimmie, run down to the store and get some beans, peas, corn, catsup and . . ."

He and Mrs. Cole ate about a quart each of the "succotash." Maxine and I sopped up a little of the juice with some bread. Afterwards, we went to the store and charged a chocolate pie and a pound of wienies, and ate sitting out on the steps.

Pop had to leave town for a few days early the next morning. He did not disturb Mrs. Cole when he left, and when we arose she was still abed. She was pretty sick, I guess, with a hangover from her "medicine," and declared pitifully that she could not arise.

"Just don't bother me, now," she whined. "Warm you up some of that nice good succotash."

Maxine and I bought some pie, soda pop and potato chips for our breakfast. We had Hershey bars and bologna for lunch. By supper time, Mrs. Cole was getting pretty hungry herself and became active long enough to open a can of chili and fry some hamburger.

Things went on like that for weeks. Pop had to be out of town the greater part of the time, and when he wasn't he spent little time at home. His mind was more than occupied with financial matters. Anyway, he had never been inclined to concern himself with family routine except on the periodic sprees I have mentioned. And those weren't much fun without Mom around.

Once in a while he would ask us how we were feeling or if we shouldn't clean up a little, but I doubt if he heard our answers. We couldn't see Mom often, and then for only a few minutes, and we were made fairly presentable for those visits.

So we went on for weeks, unfed, unwashed and in the main unschooled, for Mrs. Cole never knew whether we went or not, and the attendance laws (if there were any) were unenforced. We slept with our clothes on, a labor-saving and warmth-promoting trick Mrs. Cole had taught us. We ate almost nothing but pie, chili and hamburger. We spent our days in prowling the dime stores, seeing picture shows and loafing.

One noon while we were seated on the porch eating a lunch of pie and pop, Mom came home. She had left the hospital without the doctor's permission. She had had a premonition, she said, that she was needed at home.

Maxine and I dashed out to the taxi, jumping up and down with delight. We asked her if she was going to stay with us, and we tried to take Freddie away from her, and—and then we kind of stood back, shuffling our feet.

"What's the matter, Mom?" I said. "What you crying about?"

"N-nothing," said Mom. "Oh, you poor babies! *Where is that woman?*"

"Mrs. Cole? She's still in bed. She don't get up this early."

Mom's eyes flashed, and she brushed her nose angrily against Freddie's blanket. "Oh, doesn't she?" she said. "Well!"

She was so weak she could hardly walk, but she went up

the stairs ahead of us. She laid Freddie down on the lounge and looked around the living room. An angry moan, like that of a spurred horse, broke from her lips. She moaned again as she surveyed the filthy dining room. Glancing into the kitchen, she moaned loudest of all.

Stepping to the door of her bedroom, she drew back her fist. But she lowered it in a gentle knock, and the second knock was no more than firm.

Inside the room the bed creaked, and Mrs. Cole grunted sleepily.

"Now, you just stop botherin' me," she whined. "I told you not to call me till you seen your pappy comin'."

A terrible smile spread over Mom's face. She knocked again.

"You hear me?" called Mrs. Cole. "You want anything to eat, go down to the store an' get it. I got all I can do lookin' after myself."

Mom knocked again.

"Now you better get away from there," Mrs. Cole shouted. "Go to a pitcher show. Go down by the river an' play. Get away from there afore I come out to you!"

Mom began knocking steadily, and Mrs. Cole's warnings grew more dire. At last she arose, lumbered to the door and flung it open.

As I have indicated she was not a fast-thinking woman, and it was fixed in her mind that it was Maxine and I who had been doing the knocking. So, glaring angrily at Mom, she spoke the words that were intended for us.

"Now, you're gonna get it," she declared. "I'll warm your britches for you. You won't be able to set down for a week when—when—when—"

"Go ahead," said Mom. "Cat got your tongue?"

"W-who—who are you?"

"I'm these children's mother," said Mom. "I'm the wife of the man who hired you to look after them. I'm the wife of the man who's been paying you good money to turn my home into a pigsty. I'm the wife of the man who—I'm the—*I could murder you!*" yelled Mom.

And she damned near did.

Shrieking objurations at Mrs. Cole just to look at us kids, just to look at this house, she gave the housekeeper a kind of bearing down shake which brought her heavily to her knees. She boxed her ears, then, until her topknot came undone. And then Mom began kicking her. Mrs. Cole fell to her face and tried to crawl away, and Mom followed, kicking, giving her a crack upon the ears when the opportunity presented. Finally, her strength exhausted, she stumbled and sat down upon her.

Very wisely Mrs. Cole lay still, and Mom was sitting on her, weeping hysterically, when Pop and the doctor arrived. Pop had been out of his office when Mom left the hospital. He had hurried home as soon as he was notified of her unauthorized departure.

Mom was put to bed. The doctor examined Mrs. Cole. He had had a few words with Mom and he was an observant man. So, in Pop's presence, he told Mrs. Cole that he was slighting his duty in not reporting her to the police. Her rheumatism and other ailments were myths, he said. She had better start getting some exercise and lay off whatever she was drinking.

Mrs. Cole departed, swiftly and meekly. But her memory lingered on. It was months before Pop could acquire the nerve to interfere in household matters, and he was pretty diffident about it then.

# IX

ONE SATURDAY MORNING, a few weeks after the Cole affair, Mom, Maxine and I were eating breakfast when a polite knock sounded on our back door. Maxine and I hollered "come in" and Mom shushed us and went to answer the door.

We heard a soft voice inquire, "Begging your pardon, but do you have any work I can do?" And Mom's reply, "Well, I don't know. We can't really afford to hire anyone, right now." Then, following a heavy silence, she said, "But don't you want to come in out of the cold?"

A woman with a little boy of about four came in. Negroes. The woman was about twenty-five, and her eyes looked almost as large as her pinched, starved face. She wore only a shawl around the shoulders of her patched but spotless gingham dress, although the weather was below zero. The boy, a wizened but cheerful-looking little fellow, was little more warmly garbed.

Mom told them to sit down, and went over to the stove and got busy. That was one thing about Mom. She never wasted words when action would do the trick. She cooked them an enormous breakfast and cleared out, shooing us ahead of her. Digging back in the closets, she produced an armful of her and my discarded garments, old and outworn but still serviceable.

"Now, you just put these on before you leave," she said, when she took them into the kitchen. "You'll catch your death of cold running around the way you are!"

"Yes'm," the woman said. "Now what work do you want me to do?"

"That's all right," said Mom.

"No, ma'am. It won't be all right unless I do some work."

"Oh, well," said Mom. "You can wash the dishes if you want to."

Viola—that was the woman's name—washed the dishes. Afterwards, a little mopping-up was indicated so she mopped the floor. In so doing she got water across the threshold of the next room, so naturally that had to be mopped, too—and before it could be mopped it had to be swept, and while one was sweeping one room it was foolish to ignore another. After sweeping, the furniture had to be dusted, and . . .

Viola went to work for us.

Some relative of hers gladly took her son to board for a fraction of her wages, and Viola moved into our house. And while she was an angel, if there ever was one, she was a source of deep confusion—at least to Mom and me.

Mom had always had to be somewhat penurious to offset Pop's generosity. She had become irrevocably sharp in money matters. When she was quoted a price on an object she automatically demanded a lower one, backing the demand with derisive comments on the potential purchase. Salesgirls hid when they saw Mom coming. When a huckster or peddler stopped at our house, he usually left with a bewildered look on his face and bitter curses on his lips.

That was Mom and *that* couldn't be Mom where Viola was concerned. Viola was constantly belittling her own efforts. Mom had to scold her to keep her from working herself to death, and force presents and money upon her with naggings.

Mom became terribly upset. After a session with Viola she was apt to be kind to butchers, her pet abomination. One night when she had been skinned into accepting two pounds of bone and gristle masquerading as stew meat, Mom broke down and cried. She told Viola she was driving her crazy, and if Viola didn't "stop it" she didn't know what she was going to do.

Viola wept right along with her. She said she knew she hadn't been earning her keep, but she would do better from now on. Moreover, she had saved most of her wages, and we could have the money back.

We were a northern family by heritage, but we had lived a big part of our lives in the South, and we—we children, at least—thought southern. Hence, the reason for my puzzlement with Viola.

It was obvious even to me that she was a far superior person to Mrs. Cole. She was, in fact, the mental and moral superior of many white people I knew. But she was black, and everyone knew that Negroes were a shiftless, lazy lot who couldn't be trusted out of sight. Everyone knew that the lowest white was better than the best black.

The only way I could account for Viola's superiority was on the basis that she was part white, but this she would not admit.

"No, sir, Mister Jimmie," she laughed, when I plagued her. "I'm black, all right. All black."

"But how do you know, Viola? You might not be."

"I just know. I know the same way you know you're white."

I could not desist. Once I got some riddle on my mind, preferably one that was foolish or of no possible consequence to me, I could not expel it until it was solved.

So, in the end, I forced Viola to confess her whiteness.

She was peeling potatoes and she had just nicked her thumb with the knife. She held the bleeding digit up for me to see.

"You see there, Mister Jimmie? You don't see any white blood like that. That's all-Negro blood."

"It is not either!" I exclaimed. "That's white people's blood! It's just like mine!"

"You're joking me, Mister Jimmie."

"I am not! You're white, Viola—partly white, anyways. I guess I ought to know what white people's blood looks like!"

"I guess you should," Viola admitted in an awed voice. "Well, what do you know!"

"I knew all the time I was right," I said loftily.

Mom looked upon Viola more as a friend than a servant. But, as she was fond of saying, she didn't want friends around all the time. Thus, as she recovered her health and the economic situation improved, Viola left us for another job. Once a week, however, she returned to us for a day to give the house a good cleaning.

She did not want to take any pay for this work, but Mom always forced her to take something; if not money, some discarded clothes. As for her new employers, Viola had very little to say about them. About all we could get out of her was that they were mighty nice people, but that she'd rather be with us.

It was Pop who finally let the cat out of the bag. Not,

naturally, that he'd been trying to keep the truth from us. He just hadn't thought it of any particular consequence.

"Why, she's working for the governor," he revealed. "He gave her some little job in the mansion on my say-so, but the family liked her so well she's running the whole thing now. She—"

"The governor," said Mom, blankly. "Oh, my goodness! I've had her coming over here on her day off to sweep and scrub and—"

When Viola next appeared, Mom rebuked her for the deception, then insisted on treating her as company.

Viola didn't want to be treated as company. She just couldn't bear it, she said. And, since Mom remained firm, her visits became more and more infrequent. Finally, they stopped altogether.

We missed her terribly.

# X

HAVING ACHIEVED CONSIDERABLE success in his dual profession of attorney-accountant, Pop swiftly began to lose interest in it. That was Pop's way. He was forever advising others—notably, me—to choose one line of endeavor and stick to it, but he himself was incapable of such singleness of purpose.

Political friends who learned of his feelings offered to obtain him an appointment as United States marshal. Pop declined. They offered him a Federal judgeship. He declined that, too.

Various lucrative ventures and positions were proffered him, and he consistently turned them down. He was quite capable of making his own way in life, he stiffly averred. And during the next two- or three-odd years he set about earnestly to prove it.

I could not name all the ventures he was active in during

that period, but they included the operation of a sawmill, the proprietorship of a hotel, truck farming, running a bush-league ball club, the garbage-hauling contract for a certain Oklahoma metropolis and turkey ranching.

As each business or endeavor failed, we were left with certain mementoes of it: assets—to use the term loosely—which were at once non-liquidatable but yet, for one reason or another, impossible to discard. Thus, by the time of the demise of the turkey ranch, our residence and its environs were so encumbered that one could hardly get into it, or, once in, out.

Zoning laws and health ordinances were unheard of or unenforced in those days, else all of us would certainly have been carted off to institutions—penal or protective. As it was, Mom finally became hysterical. She declared that she herself would see to Pop's commitment if he did not come to his senses.

"G-garbage wagons!" she wept. "G-garbage wagons in the front yard, and—a-and h-horses in the garage, a-and ploughs on the front porch, a-and—"

She went on with her recital, becoming more and more agitated with the mention of each item. The incubators in the bedrooms. The gangsaws in the living room. The cigar showcases in the kitchen. The tomato plants in the bathroom. The dozens of newly hatched young turkeys, which roamed the house from one end to the other. The—

"And that ball player!" yelled Mom. "I swear, Jim Thompson, if you don't get him out of here, I'll—I'll murder both of you!"

This last reference was to the occupant of our sleeping porch, a rheumy old party who combined an affection for chewing tobacco with very poor eyesight. He could not have hit a bull with a bass fiddle, as the saying is. Pop, of course, perversely regarded him as a second Ty Cobb.

"You get him out of here!" Mom shouted. "Get all this

junk away from here. Either he and it goes or the children and I do!"

Pop gave in, not, naturally, because he could be swayed by threats, but because he was quite as weary of the situation as Mom was. He found some political sinecure for the ball player, and gave away the other animals and items. Good riddance it was—as none knew better than he. But you could never make him admit it.

For years, nay decades, no visitor came to our house without learning that Pop had once owned a very valuable ball player ("another Babe Ruth") or some very valuable horses ("the same blood strain as Man O' War") or several hundred prize turkeys ("their eggs were worth a hundred dollars a dozen"). To hear Pop tell it, he had been on the point of cornering the world market in tomatoes or timber or hotel gaboons ("genuine antiques, mind you"). All the nominal dross which Mom had forced him to get shed of had actually been gold, and only her callous and ignorant interference had prevented his reaping untold wealth.

"Of course," he would sigh bravely, in concluding his recital, "I don't blame Mrs. Thompson in the least. It was my own fault for listening to her."

He would laugh hollowly, then, his face fixed in a stoical mask. And while Mom choked and stammered incoherently, our guests would stare at her open-mouthed, pity and horror mingling in their eyes.

Of necessity, and as much as it irked him, Pop had continued to practice law and accountancy. But he was constantly on the lookout for some new field of activity, and he finally found it, or so he felt, in the booming Oklahoma oil fields.

I mentioned a few pages back that his first dabblings in this business were not too successful. This, on reflection, seems an unfair statement of the case. They were successful enough, but Pop's generosity and trustingness turned them into failures.

On one occasion, after several shrewd deals, he gave a "friend" twenty-five thousand dollars to tie up some leases for him. Instead, the man bought an automobile agency and placed it in his wife's name. There was nothing Pop could do about it. The law regards such an action as a breach of trust, and its attitude briefly is that anyone who suffers it has only himself to blame.

Another time, Pop accepted the word and the handshake of a pipeline executive in lieu of a written contract. As a result, when the pipeline company found it inexpedient to connect with his first oil well, he could only let the torrent of black gold pour into the nearest creek.

It was a few months after this last fiasco, when Pop was again hard at work at his now-detested law-accountancy practice, that he met a man named Jake Hamon. Or, I should say, re-met him. For he had known him casually during his early days in Oklahoma. At that time, Jake, a former roustabout with the Ringling Brothers Circus, had been a six-for-fiver around the pioneer tent and shack towns. That is, he bought wages from workers in advance of their due date, giving the needy borrower five dollars for each six he had coming.

Jake was still in the loan business at the time of his and Pop's later encounter, though on a slightly different level. He owned a string of Oklahoma banks. He also owned a railroad, oil wells, refineries, office buildings—so much, in fact, that he had acquired the sobriquet of "John D. Rockefeller of the Southwest."

He asked Pop to audit his banks and to equip them with a more efficient accounting system. Pop, having nothing better to do, gladly agreed.

"I won't charge you anything, of course," he said, casually. "Just my expenses."

"Why?" Jake demanded.

"Well"—Pop was a little set back. His generous offers were not usually received in this fashion. "Well, after all we're old friends and—"

Jake interrupted him with a rude four-letter ejaculation. "Who the hell says we're friends?" he snarled. "I haven't seen you in years, and if you're as big a dope as you act like I don't want to see you again. Friends, hell! I've heard about some of your friends. Forget that friend crap. Name me a fee for this job, or get the hell out of my office!"

Smarting, Pop named him a fee—one that was outrageously high. And Jake chortled happily.

"You see?" he grinned. "All you need is a tough guy like me to ride herd on you. You stick with me, Jim, and you'll wear diamonds."

So Pop went to work for Jake, and for the first time in his life he held on to a large share of the money he made. The relation of the two men, at first, was that of employer and employee. From that it shifted to a point where Pop was Jake's advisor on various deals, at a percentage of the profits. And in the end they became partners in the deals—usually oil—with Jake providing the lion's share of the money and Pop carrying out the necessary negotiations. Pop became a familiar figure at lease auctions and distress sales. The transactions were frequently cash on the barrelhead. And on at least one occasion Pop's briefcase contained a million dollars of Jake's money.

While Pop made and continued to make a great deal of money with Jake, "the Southwest's Rockefeller" himself profited vastly by the association. Even as he watched over Pop, so did Pop watch over him, checking the ugly temper and cynical attitude which, as Jake would surlily admit, had cost him millions and made him a public-relations man's headache.

Unfortunately, no one likes to be reminded of his faults, real and harmful as they may be. And the closer their association became and the greater their familiarity, the more flaws they found with one another. Nothing that the other did was right. Pop was a "softie," Jake an "illiterate boor." Jake was a "slob," Pop a "high-toned dude." So it went.

Since Pop was genuinely fond of Jake, and vice versa, and both had given concrete proof of that liking, it always seemed incredible to me that they could have come to a parting of the ways.

Pop refused to talk about the breakup for a long time. When he finally did explain, I could only sit and gape, for the *casus belli* had been a suit of underwear.

It had happened—the breakup—in the sweltering hotel room of an Oklahoma boom town. They were there, pending the closing of a business deal, and during their stay Jake's mistress had arrived. He got her a room across the hall from theirs, and spent the nights with her. During the day he stayed in his and Pop's room, conferring upon business matters.

It was hot, as I have said. He seldom wore anything but his underwear. And one morning, when he was prowling restlessly about their room, he surprised Pop in a disgusted frown.

"What's the matter with you?" he inquired gruffly.

"I was about to ask you the same thing," Pop retorted.

"What do you mean? What are you staring at, anyway?"

"Since you asked me," said Pop, coldly, "I was looking at your underclothes. When was the last time you changed them?"

"Why, you—" Jake's face turned scarlet. "You two-bit bookkeeper, I ought to—!"

He exploded into a torrent of abuse.

Pop replied similarly.

Before they could see the ridiculousness of the situation and get control of themselves, each had said unforgivable—or at least unforgettable—things and their partnership was ended.

They saw one another after that, but there was a certain stiffness between them. And Pop had reason to suspect—or felt he had—that Jake still bore a grudge against him.

Next, Pop lost almost ten thousand dollars in a poker game with Jake, Gaston B. Means and Warren G. Harding.

The game took place on the Harding presidential campaign train, upon which, as two of the Southwest's most prominent Republicans, Pop and Jake were guests of honor. It began with relatively low stakes which Jake, with much jibing and jeering, managed to steadily increase. Finally, with all the cash available in the pot, Means dropped out, and the contest was between Jake, Harding and Pop. In other words, since Pop was too stiffnecked and proud to demand a table-stakes game, it was no contest.

Jake could write his check for any amount. And certainly the I.O.U. of a future president was good for any amount. Only Pop's betting was restricted.

He tossed in his hand, a club flush. Immediately, although he had anted heavily on the previous round, Jake laid down his hand—the value of which was absolutely nothing. Harding took the pot with three threes.

Pop was considerably, if not justifiably, irritated. He did not see Jake again until some two years later when the latter summoned him to his death bed. Then, with matters past mending, they sadly agreed that the biggest mistake of their lives had been the ending of their association.

Pop, feeling that Oklahoma was not big enough for the two of them, had transferred his activities to Texas. And there he had drilled four oil-less oil wells in a row, at a cost of more than two hundred thousand dollars each.

Jake, sans any friendly restraint or guidance, had become increasingly misanthropic, and, finally, his mistress took a gun to him and he died of the wounds.

# XI

WE MOVED TO FORT WORTH, Texas, in the fall of 1919, shortly before the coming of my thirteenth birthday. The city was riding a tidal wave of postwar wealth. New building was months behind the demand, and there were a dozen purchasers for every available house. So, for several weeks, we were forced to live in a hotel suite. The period was one of the most unpleasant in my checkered career.

For the first time in my memory, I was immediately under Pop's eye day in and day out. And Pop, who had taken only a spasmodic interest in me until then, now began to make up for lost time. I was a rich man's son, he pointed out, and some day I would inherit great wealth. I must be made into a proper custodian for it—sane, sober, considerate. I should not be allowed to become one of those ill-mannered, irresponsible wastrels, who behaved as though they had been put on earth solely to enjoy themselves.

No error in my deportment was too tiny for Pop to spot and criticize. No flaw in my appearance was too small. From the time I arose until the time I retired, I was subjected to a steady stream of criticism about the way I dressed, walked, talked, stood, ate, sat, and so on into infinity—all with that most maddening of assurances that it was for my "own good."

We had two cars in the hotel garage. Pop took me there and placed me under the supervision of the foreman mechanic, instructing him to treat me as he would any hired hand. For the ensuing week I assisted in the overhauling of our automobiles. Rather, I did the overhauling with some minor assistance from one of the mechanics. I was too outraged and sullen to discuss the work, so I did not dispute Pop's bland statement that the experience would teach me a great deal. For that matter, it did teach me a great deal— namely, that repairing cars was a lousy way to make a living. And never again, except in the direst emergencies, did I so much as change a tire.

Always in the past, Mom had served as a bulwark against Pop's extremes of family management, but she proved remiss in this emergency, a fact decidedly less puzzling in retrospect than it was at the time. Pop had behaved intelligently—instead of with his sporadic brilliance—throughout his partnership with Jake Hamon, and she was naturally inclined to regard his intense interest in me as a continuation of that intelligent behavior. Moreover, say what you will, it is difficult to dispute the judgment of a man who has made a million dollars.

I was finally impelled to dispute it, in fact to raise holy hell about it, when Pop took me to buy my school clothes, the chief item of which was a blue-serge knickerbocker suit with velvet-braided lapels and pearl buttons. I had not used any profanity in years—and never in front of Pop whose nearest approach to cursing was an occasional darn or gosh. But now I cut loose. Before I could be dragged out of the swank men's clothing store, the swallow-tailed clerks were fleeing for cover, their manicured fingers stoppering their scarlet ears.

I was returned to the hotel and confined to my room. As further punishment, I was advised that I would not be allowed to accompany the family on a tour of the oil fields, but would remain in Fort Worth in the custody of Pa.

I advised the family—at the top of my lungs—that they could all go to hell.

Pa had joined us in Fort Worth with the announced intention of getting us settled, but actually, I am sure, as a way of getting away from Ma. He had given me none of the support I expected in my skirmishes with Pop, and I was thoroughly disgusted with him. Pa—the orphan—said that I was damned lucky to have a smart man like Pop looking after me. He said that it was every man's right to make a damned fool of himself, and that my turn would come later.

I was disgusted with Pa. I felt that he had failed me sorely. Thus, the following morning, when he came into my room after the family's departure, I told him to get the hell out.

"Have a smoke," said Pa, tossing me a foot-long Pittsburgh stogie. "Got a little surprise for you."

The surprise, or part of it, arrived right behind him: a white-jacketed waiter with a pitcher of boiling water, a bowl of lemons and sugar. Pa took a bottle of bootleg corn whiskey from his hip and mixed us two tremendous hot toddies.

"Kind of like old times, ain't it?" he said, slanting his savagely humorous old eyes at me. "You remember that night out by the privy when— Now, what the hell you sniveling about, anyway?"

"I—n-nothing," I said, choking back a sob.

"Light up, then. Drink up. Stop acting like a goddamned calf. Anything I hate to see it's a fella cryin' in good whiskey."

I lit up and drank up. The steam from the toddies mingled with the clouds of cigar smoke, and the morning sunlight shone through it upon Pa's bald head. It seemed to me he wore a halo.

"I tell you somethin', Jimmie," he said casually, freshening our drinks from the bottle. "We all got our own way of doin' things, an' that's the way we got to do 'em. Ain't no man can do a thing another fella's way. Ain't no use tryin' to make him. He'll just go his own way all the harder, an' he'll be your enemy besides."

I nodded my understanding, although I was far from agreeing with his doctrine. Pa went on to remark that while other people had their ways, he also had his, and it was no more than just and proper that he should pursue that way since I had been left in his charge.

"In other words," he concluded, "anyone that thinks you're going to tag around with me in that outfit your Pop bought you has got another goddamned think coming."

He gave me another stogie and urged me to help myself to a second toddy. Then, he left the room, returning a few minutes later with one of his "uniforms"—complete even to the wide-brimmed black hat and Congress gaiters. All that was missing was the cane, and Pa promised to pick one up for me if I felt too naked without it.

Happily, the stogie lodged in the corner of my mouth, I dressed.

The hat and the gaiters had to be stuffed with paper to be wearable. And since Pa stood six feet to my five and weighed two hundred pounds to my one-ten, the suit was a trifle large. But this difficulty was easily solved—to our satisfaction at least. The pants legs were rolled up and under

for a few inches, likewise the coat sleeves. A few pins here
and there and the job was done.

True, the seat of the pants bagged to my knees, but the
coat reached below them. One hand washed the other, to use
Pa's metaphor. I looked fine, he declared, and no one but a
damned fool would think otherwise. So, equipped with fresh
stogies, we sallied forth.

During my long residence in Fort Worth, I often felt that it
was cursed with more than its share of damned fools. But it
was a western city, and peculiarities of dress went more unmarked than otherwise. Thus, while I drew a number of
startled glances, no one, damned fool or otherwise, said or
did anything about me.

Pa and I ate a whopping breakfast of steak, eggs and hot
cakes, and only once did he see fit to criticize me. That was
when he observed me eating from the sharp edge of my
knife, and he pointed out the danger of it, suggesting that I
use the reverse edge instead.

After breakfast we went to a pool hall where Pa beat me
five games of slop pool and I beat him two. We returned to
the hotel, then, for a few before-lunch drinks, and following
lunch we went to a penny arcade.

Pa had brought the bottle with him, and he became quite
rambunctious when "A Night With A Paris Cutie" did not
come up to his expectations. He caned the machine. I think
he would have caned the arcade proprietor, but that shrewd
gentleman wisely gave him no back talk. Instead, he returned Pa's coins and led him out to the sidewalk. He
pointed to a burlesque house across and down the street.

"Why look at pictures," he inquired, "when you can see
the real thing?"

"Well, now," said Pa, greatly mollified. "Maybe you got
something there, friend."

Fort Worth had a number of burlesque houses at that time,
and we were able to obtain choice seats on the front or

"baldhead" row. Except for three brief and alternate absences, we stayed there until the house closed at midnight.

Those absences? Well, first I went outside to buy a cane so that I could hook the girls on the ramp as Pa did. Then, Pa went out for a fresh supply of whiskey. Then, I went out for a carton of coffee and sandwiches.

It was a wonderfully satisfying day. Pa had given a bottle to the ushers and sent a couple of others backstage, and in that place he and I could do no wrong. We hooked the girls' garments until they were reduced to near nudity. Pa climbed upon the ramp and chased them backstage. Yet they responded with laughter and joyous shrieks, and occasionally one would stoop swiftly and plant a kiss on Pa's head.

Each of the succeeding three days, at the end of which the family returned, was a reasonable facsimile of that first day. Hot toddies in the morning, then a pool game, then a burlesque house, with drinks and meals being imbibed at strategic intervals. Also much talk from Pa, much advice delivered in his casual back-handed fashion.

I am afraid that most of what he said was wasted upon me. But I was imbued with a little of his wisdom, at least briefly. I gave Pop no further argument about the clothes, and I submitted silently if sullenly to his criticisms. For a time, I was docile.

Then we bought a house and Pa returned to Nebraska and I started to school.

Texas had only eleven grades of school as compared with the twelve in other states. Thus, as an eighth-grade student in the Oklahoma schools, I was technically a first-year high-school student in Texas. Being extremely praise-hungry, and anxious to shine in Pop's eyes, I took advantage of that technicality.

Nowadays, it is no unusual thing for a twelve-year-old—and I was still twelve—to enter high school. But it was unusual at that time. More important, in my case, it was completely unjustifiable.

I had read voraciously and far in advance of my years, and I was a walking compendium of largely unassimilated knowledge drilled into me by Pop. But I was sadly prepared for the inelastic high-school curriculum. In our various moves from place to place, I had been absent from grammar school practically as much as I had attended. Now, I was missing a whole year. I knew nothing of cube and square root and many other things upon which the high-school subjects were predicated.

Despite the sorry state of my elementary schooling, I think I might have done passably in the higher grades if I could have put my heart into it. I have almost always managed to do the things I really cared about doing. Similarly, however, and doubtless regrettably, I can do nothing at all if I do not care. And I become uncaring very quickly if I am prodded or driven, or if the people involved are distasteful to me.

To put the last thing first, the Texans were distasteful—or so I soon convinced myself. I studied their mannerisms and mores, and in my twisted outlook they became Mongoloid monsters. I saw all their bad and no offsetting good.

Texans made boast of their insularism; they bragged about such things as never having been outside the state or the fact that the only book in their house was the Bible. Texans did not need to work to improve their characters as Pop was constantly pressing me to do. All Texans were born with perfect characters, and these became pluperfect as their owners drank the unrivaled Texas waters, breathed the wondrous Texas air and trod the holy Texas soil.

Texas, it appeared, had formed all but a minuscule part of the Confederacy, and as such had slapped the troops of Sherman silly and sent Grant's groaning to their graves.

Singlehanded—almost, anyway—it had thrashed the bully, North. Then, as a generous though intrinsically meaningless gesture, it had conceded defeat, thus ending the awful bloodshed and preserving the Union.

Just as all Texas males were omnipotent, invincible and of irreproachable character, so were all Texas women superbly beautiful and utterly virginal. And woe to anyone who hinted the contrary. Being of an open mind (by my own admission), I was willing to concede that the Texas female was probably somewhat more personable than a Ubangi, but I would make no concessions on the second score. I delighted in pointing out the historic incompatibility of virginity with wife- and mother-hood. Mock-innocent, I demanded that the peculiar Texas situation be explained to me. As a rule, my heretical quizzing was rewarded at this point with a punch in the nose; if not, I would extend the questioning into the sacrosanct realm of Texas sweethearts and sisters.

That, invariably, would get me not one punch but a dozen.

Anything that a Texan might be sensitive about or hold sacred, I jeered at. There was no trick too low for me if it would discomfit the Texans.

I recall—and it makes me squirm to do it—the pleased astonishment of the coach when I applied for a place on the high-school track team. How unselfishly delighted he was that I was at last coming out of my shell. I recall his almost tearful joy as I skimmed tirelessly and swiftly around the track—a half mile, mile, mile-and-a-half, two miles. I was a natural-born two-miler, he declared—rangy, wiry, long legged. I was the best two-miler he had ever seen, and he hugged me ecstatically. The two-mile event was in the bag. If only he had a few more lads like me!

It was a damned good thing for him that he didn't have any more like me, for, while I represented our school in the intramural two-mile race, I did not run it.

I trotted up in front of the grandstand, sat down in the middle of the track and lighted a cigarette.

Only my tender years, I suspect, saved me from being lynched.

# XII

I HAD NOT completely plumbed the abyss of ignominy when I came under the influence of a Boy Scout leader, and for a time my descent was checked. Then, suddenly and inexplicably, he became cool and critical, and I resumed my career of making everyone else as miserable as I was.

Years later, when I was shaking out of the grandfather of all hangovers, Pop tried to get at the root of my trouble.

"I just can't understand it," he complained. "I can't see how it started. You were always such a bright, likeable, willing youngster. So well-balanced and adaptable."

"I was, huh?" I laughed hoarsely. "Well, well."

"Of course you were! Why, your scoutmaster made a special trip to my office to tell me about you. He said you were the finest boy in his troop."

"Don't kid me," I said. "That guy got me to liking him,

69

then he turned on me and he never gave me a pleasant word from then on."

"Now, I wonder why he did that." Pop frowned in honest puzzlement. "I believe I did tell him that praise could be very bad for a boy, and that I hoped you wouldn't acquire a swelled head. But surely——"

Well.

I was easily the most unpopular student in school. Also, it goes without saying, I was the poorest student. I had read all the standard historians, Gibbon, Wells, even Herodotus, yet I could not—rather, would not—pass the Texas history courses. I had read a complete twelve-volume botanical encyclopedia, but I failed in botany. I had read Ibanez's *Mare Nostrum* as well as some of Alarcon's shorter plays in their original language, yet I failed in Spanish. I had sold fillers to the pulp periodicals and brief humorous squibs to such magazines as *Judge*, but I failed in English. Most thoroughly, I failed in algebra and geometry, two subjects which struck me as so wholly nonsensical that they were *beneath*, beneath contempt—if you follow my meaning.

In one of my softer moments, I proposed a bargain to my math teacher: if she would prove to me that her chosen subjects were not as stupid as I claimed, then I would study them. She did not take me up on the offer, and she seemed very embittered by it. The good woman gave me what is doubtless the lowest grade ever meted out to a student—not just a zero, but zero-minus.

I was a high-school freshman at twelve. Almost six years later I was still a high-school freshman. From being the youngest I became the oldest, from being a beardless stripling I grew into manhood (junior grade). Strangers to the school often mistook me for a member of the faculty.

I was expelled and suspended so many times for disobedience, refusing to study, cutting classes, playing truant, et cetera, that I lost track of them. So also did the school.

Suspensions were piled upon expulsions and expulsions upon suspensions, so that the harried records clerk never knew when I was legitimately present or illegally absent. Along toward the last, just before she gave up the unequal struggle with my status, I overheard the tag end of her plea to one of my teachers, " . . . please do not suspend him until he is reinstated from expulsion so I can suspend him as of last month so I can reinstate him to be expelled, so—s-so— *I'M G-GOING C-CRAAA-ZY!*"

Now and then, sometimes for the better part of a term, I escaped into the upper classes. But inevitably my scholastic record would catch up with me, and I would be returned to the freshman fold. One term, having received so many lectures that I had begun to fear for my hearing, I decided to try to reform. I promoted myself into the senior class. There, where I rightfully should have been had I behaved as I should have, I was polite to the teachers and I studied as I had never studied before. My grades soared higher and higher. As the end of the term neared, I was placed in that select group of students whose marks were so good that they were excused from final examinations.

When finally they were apprised of my status, my teachers were incredulous. They had had no dealings with me before that term, and they could not believe that I was the James Thompson who had established an all-time record for boorishness and boobery. Unfortunately, there was indisputable proof that the onerous and ornery James was one and the same with theirs. So, since I lacked the prerequisite courses, my brilliant term's work availed me nothing. I received no credit hours for it.

I was right back where I had started, still a freshman.

Despite my chagrin and disappointment, I did not feel that my work had been entirely wasted. For one thing, I had rid myself of a worrisome suspicion that I was as stupid as most people thought. For another, I had been made to see the inexorable crux of my problem.

Obviously, mere study and better behavior were not going to get me out of high school. Not, that is, within a reasonable time. No matter how hard I studied nor how well I behaved, I would still have to spend four more years in school on top of the approximately six years I had already served. The records would force me to.

So there was the problem, not in me, as I saw it, but in the records.

Something would have to be done about them.

At this time, and for some time prior to it, I was employed as a night bellboy in a large hotel. The list of my acquaintances extended into places which, in my present pious state, gives me shivers to think about. A Square Sam myself, I was known to be "strictly okay" and a "right kid." In no time at all I was in touch with a burglar, explaining my problem and asking his help on a fee basis.

"I dunno, kid," he said, scratching his head doubtfully. "I'd like to help you out, but—well, I just dunno."

"But it's a cinch," I said. "The stuff isn't in a safe. All you have to do is pick the locks on a couple doors. Then, you get rid of my record card and fill in one of their blanks. I'll tell you just what to put on it, and—"

"I don't know nothing about those things, kid. I'd foul it up for you, sure."

"Don't do anything to it, then. Just get rid of the record and bring me one of the blanks and—"

"Huh-uh. I go into a place once, I'm through with it. I don't go back no more. Anyway, suppose they look for that card and it ain't there. They'd come down on you like a ton of bricks, kid."

"Well"—I hesitated—"how about this? Take someone with you that—"

"Look, kid!" He held up a hand. "You just don't do things

that way. A guy's a penman, he don't do nothing else. He wouldn't touch a burglary for love or money. There's only one way to do this job. Get to the party that keeps the records. Put a fix in with her."

"She's not on the take," I said glumly. "I know that dame!"

"Well," he shrugged, "that's the way you'll have to swing it. If you can't do it from the inside, you just ain't gonna get it done."

I left him disconsolately, all the more depressed because I knew he was right. A new record card, filled out in a hand wholly dissimilar to that of the other cards, would be damnably incriminating. Even with a fix in, the crime was certain to be spotted. For as long as school was in session the cards were referred to, and there were certain teachers who knew my record by heart.

I had not one problem, then, but two. To do the job from the inside, and to do it right at the close of the school term. Thus, by the time there was again occasion to refer to that card, I would be safely out of reach, my sins would have become dim in the minds of the authorities, and any long-memoried snoop who sought to make trouble would find his contentions impossible to prove.

It was a large order, one seemingly impossible to fill. Yet fill it I must or become the world's only senile schoolboy.

So fill it I did. And I shall tell you how I did it a little later.

Meanwhile, let us move back in the story, taking its events in as proper a sequence as their general impropriety will permit.

# XIII

OP'S LUCK WENT sour almost from the day he set foot in Texas. The fortune which I was to inherit shrank at the rate of almost four hundred thousand dollars a year. I naturally thought it was a hell of a note to be losing all that dough without so much as a soda to show for it, but I was more concerned with certain issues tangential to the main one. Briefly, as I discussed them with Pop, they were about as follows:

First of all, was a man who had made such a thorough screw-up of his own affairs a suitable mentor for me? (I did not think so.)

Second, with him losing money at the rate of a couple thousand dollars a week, was there any sense in my knocking myself out for a pittance on some part-time job? (I did not think so.)

Finally, since I apparently would have no dough to look

after, wasn't all this Spartan training I was undergoing pretty damned stupid? (I thought it was.)

I was not trying to be snide or facetious, and I was irritated and bewildered that Pop should think I was. I pointed out that if I wanted to be smart-alecky or nasty, I could do a heck of a lot better than that. ("Just ask anyone, Pop.") But Pop was as near to being furious as I have ever seen him.

Addressing me as "sirrah," he let it be known that I was pretty poor comfort for a man no longer young whose life's gleanings were slipping through his fingers, never to be grasped again. He said that when he was my age he had done such and such and so and so, and all I could do was get into trouble and sass my betters. He said that I was completely irresponsible and out-of-hand, and that the remedy lay in work and more work. He had been too easy-going with me, he said, but now the old free and easy days were over.

I was to study every night from dinner until bedtime. Also, since I had chosen to quit my part-time job as a soda jerk, I would find "suitable" employment on the weekends.

The first ordinance did not bother me particularly. I was no more popular in the neighborhood than I was elsewhere, and normally remained indoors at night for reasons connected with my health. I did not study, naturally, but the fact was difficult to prove. I was always writing something. I always had a half-dozen books spread in front of me. They never had anything to do with my lessons, but Pop would have been the first to argue the fact. *The Prince*, to his way of thinking, was a splendid and necessary adjunct to the study of civics. So also was there an indisputable relationship between Schopenhauer and sociology, Malthus and mathematics, and Lycurgus and commercial law.

It was easy, then, to meet Pop's "study" requirements. But finding part-time work was something else again. Such employment was difficult to find in that day, and it paid very little when one did find it. It will seem incomprehensible to our contemporary youth, who sneer at offers of a five-dollar fee for mowing a lawn, but my wage as a soda-jerk had been five dollars for an approximate thirty-hour week.

Pop was a firm believer in the adage that there is always work for those who want it, and when I found none in the time allotted me, he supplied it. He bought a ladder, brushes, and a supply of paint and set me to work painting the house.

Now, while I showed little liking for useful employment, it does not necessarily follow that I liked useless work any better. And this was worse than useless. The house was only a few months old. It stood in need of paint much less than I. Disgusted and resentful, I did the job at the rate of a few inches a day, painting over and over the same places. The end effect, naturally, was that of a checker board, and the whole place had to be done over by professional painters.

We lived in an unincorporated suburb of Fort Worth. Like our neighbors—a meat packer, a steel magnate and another oil man—we had bought the lots surrounding ours, and our total land holdings were probably an acre. Pop now caused a barn to be built on this surplus land, and furnished it with two purebred Jerseys. And I, I was advised, was in the dairy business.

Since we were outside the city limits, our neighbors were without legal recourse. Mom, her frugal soul mollified by the prospect of free milk for the household, did no more than hint that Pop had become a hopeless lunatic. I protested, of course, bitterly, profanely and continuously. And knowing something of Pop you will know how little my protests accomplished.

I was to have full charge of the cows—"a free hand," as Pop put it. The family would receive its milk free, the remainder would be distributed through a house-to-house milk route, which would be "no trouble at all" for me to establish.

I would be allowed to keep any monies remaining—after the care and feeding of the cows had been paid for.

"It's a wonderful opportunity for you," said Pop. "You should be very grateful."

I said something that sounded like "ship."

Not that I gave a damn really, but there were no profits from the business. Jerseys are not the hardiest breed of cattle, and one visit from a veterinarian consumed the returns from a week's sale of milk. Too, while customers were fairly plentiful in the beginning, they did not continue so. They seemed alarmed by a milkman who lost no opportunity to declare that he would be fried with onions sooner than touch a drop of that "blank blank triple-blank Jersey juice."

I put up with the dairy until summer. Then, being told that I would have to keep the cows staked out during the day— move them around on a tether from one vacant lot to another—I went down to the railroad yards and caught a northbound freight.

I got as far as Kansas before I was apprehended and returned.

I waited a few days, then caught a freight southward.

I was brought back from Houston.

Pop sold the cows.

I was made to feel, of course, that I had behaved very badly. The family had been put to much expense and trouble, on my account, and the only return I would give them was insolence and shiftlessness.

I was bewildered by this attitude, and still am. Even more now than I was at the time.

I have three children, one a fifteen-year-old boy. I think they are pretty good kids, but honesty compels me to say that no one of them has ever made a bed, washed a dish or swept a floor without violent protest. Moreover, they commonly refer to their mother and me as "nuts" or "screwy" and they frequently suggest that we "turn blue" or "stop breathing" or otherwise end our patent misery.

You see, when these children were quite young we had an elderly man living with us. This man would not let the children lift a finger to any task, reproaching us scornfully and speaking darkly of "child slaves." He would not let us reprove them, no matter what their misdeeds. He sternly ruled down the suggestions that treats should be withheld for bad behavior, and that allowances should be earned with household chores. Naturally, the kids got pretty spoiled.

Who was this man, you ask? Who was the man who encouraged our children in insolence, who constantly bawled us out for failing to swallow his dictum that kids were kids and should only be addressed with words of praise?

Who?

Pop.

# XIV

WE SPENT A large part of that summer at the fashion-
able Spa, in Waukesha, Wisconsin. The family
lounged about the place "taking the waters," and I
found employment as a plumber's helper. I did not mind it
too much.

Jack, the plumber I was assigned to, was a prize gold-
brick, a man who saw no virtue in work whatsoever. "I can
lay right down aside a job and go to sleep," he would boast.
He seldom referred to work as such, apparently hating even
the sound of it. He spoke of it rather with a kind of glum
obliqueness as "the Killer."

He struck me as being an extremely wise and discerning
man, and I treated him with due deference. Under his earnest tutelage, I became almost as expert at stalling and loafing as he.

One morning, the morning after a day we had killed in

repairing a leaky toilet trap, the boss plumber confronted Jack with considerable severity.

He said that he had put up with just about all he was going to, and that he would be "forced to take steps" unless Jack improved his ways.

Jack blinked at him stolidly. Then he reached into an inside pocket, took out a notebook and withdrew a sheaf of clippings from it.

"Read those," he commanded.

The boss read them, perforce. They were all obituaries of people who had died while working.

"'At's what you're up to," Jack would growl, at the conclusion of each clipping. "You tryin' to kill me, maybe?"

There was obviously but one acceptable answer to the question, and the boss made it over and over. In fact, as Jack glowered and glared at him, his huge hands fondling a thirty-six-inch Stillson, our employer began to anticipate the gloomy inquiry. He could not stand it if anything happened to us, he babbled. We must take better care of ourselves and avoid over-exertion in the summer heat.

Jack finally allowed him to escape to his office. Whereupon, of course, my colleague placed his hands on his hips, spread his feet, sucked in his lungs, threw back his head, opened his mouth to its widest, and addressed the ceiling with a bellowed promise to kill that dirty son-of-a-bitch.

Along with obituaries of people who had succumbed to "the Killer," Jack collected French postcards, and many was the hour we whiled away with these in the restfully cool sanctuary of bathrooms, basements and cess-basins.

"Looky at them," Jack would say. "Now, ain't that somethin'?"

"Now, ain't that somethin'!" I would respond.

"Betcha they's plenty o' people'd give a thousand dollars to see somethin' like that."

"Betcha they *is* plenty."

Jack felt there was an unreasonable and foolish prejudice against these "art studies" and that a fortune awaited the person who could overcome it.

"Everyone likes 'em themselves," he said, "but they're afraid to let on. Now, if you could get everyone to lookin' at 'em all at the same time, out in the open like—"

"Yeah," I frowned wisely. "All at the same time. Out in the open like."

Jack was much impressed with the manner in which I held up my end of our discussions. He said I had a way of getting right to the point of a thing, and that I did wonders toward clarifying his own thinking.

We were installing guard rails in a local food-processing plant when the solution to the French-postcard-prejudice problem came to him. Generous man that he was, and grateful for the many times I had gotten to the point of things, he promised me a full half of his potential millions.

"Yes, sir, Jimmie," he said, nodding to a conveyor belt. "That's the way to do it. We hit the nail right on the head."

"Yes, sir," I said, blankly. "That's the way to do it."

"Them packages."

"Them packages."

"We slip 'em in there."

"We slip— Hey!" I said. "What are we waiting for?"

It seemed odd that this triumphant moment should have marked the beginning of the end of a beautiful friendship. But I am forced to report that it did. For now instead of plunging forthright into the cause, and forging ahead to victory and riches, Jack held back in ultra-caution. We had to do the thing right, he said. And they was plenty of things to be worked out before we could do it right.

As the days passed, and two items appeared in the ranks of things-to-be-worked-out for each one I expunged, I became impatient with Jack, then suspicious of him. I declared that he was deliberately delaying operations until I had returned to Texas where I would be unable to reap my just dues as co-owner of the company.

Jack was placatory for a time. But I seemed to detect a certain lack of candor in his manner—a damning sheepishness. So my indictments continued, and finally he was brought to respond with hideous slurs. He said I was an eager beaver, willing and willful fodder for "the Killer." He would bet money, he said, that I *liked* to work; he had had his doubts about me from the beginning, and my vigorous manner and unseemly impetuosity had now revealed the awful truth to him.

We stopped speaking after that.

We did not speak again until the eve of my departure for Texas, when we shook hands diffidently and exchanged stiff farewells.

More than thirty years have passed since that stilly evening in a Wisconsin plumbing shop. Thirty years, in which I have become the noninventing inventor of such things as story-book toilet paper, cigarettes with built-in matches, neckties which assume the hue of the gravy dropped on them and a tongue-shaped sponge for licking stamps. So I can understand Jack's attitude now. I can see that the more beautiful a dream, the more hopeless its realization, that we have but to grasp to destroy it.

All I could see at the time, however, was that a venal and crafty man had taken sorry advantage of an innocent and trusting boy. And for months after our return to Texas, I searched for proof of Jack's perfidy.

Every container of food that came into the house was carefully dissected by me—cartons, labels, wrappers, tax stamps. I even took apart the lids of catsup bottles and cracked open the stoppers to sauce carafes. Since I declined to explain this activity, mumbling only of a million dollars and people who thought they could kid me, the family was more than ever convinced that I didn't have a brain in my head.

Which, I imagine, was a pretty fair statement of the case.

# XV

THE SCHOOL I attended was not too far distant from Glen Garden Country Club, so it was only natural that I should gravitate there in search of week-end employment. I found it, as a caddie, and I liked it. At least, I liked it better than the other types of work I had thus far encountered. There was something about receiving pay from play which pleased me very much. And, as a Glen Garden caddie, one had the privilege of playing on the course at certain hours.

You were out at the club at the crack of dawn, you and Ben Hogan and Byron Nelson, and all the other caddies who were ambitious to improve "their game." There wasn't a full set of clubs among the lot of you, but that didn't matter. You formed into foursomes, according to your handicap. You strode down the dew-wet fairway, calling back and forth to one another, diagnosing each other's drives and approaches as competently as any pro. Later in the day, when the jobs were being passed out, you would engage in profane and bloody struggle behind the caddie shack. But now all the niceties of etiquette were observed. All was politeness and consideration.

The game made you that way.

I thought it was pretty swell.

Well, though, caddies were paid sixty-five cents for eighteen holes, and there were more caddies than there were those who wanted them. On a good day, during a tournament for example, you might "get out" twice for a total of thirty-six holes. And if the tips broke right for you, you might make as much as a dollar seventy-five or two dollars. This was darned big money, of course, for a mere twelve or fifteen miles' trudging with a fifty-pound bag on your back. But it was seldom that one enjoyed such great good fortune.

On an average, you were lucky to get out for eighteen. Or maybe a round and nine. And there were days when you waited around from dawn to sunset without ever getting out. Obviously, as Pop pointed out, caddying was neither dependable nor lucrative.

He did not forbid me to continue with it. In fact, although my habit of ellipsis may have made him appear otherwise, Pop very seldom ordered me or forbade me to do anything. Pop believed in "reasoning a thing through," in "looking at a matter from all sides." There were times, as I have indicated, when I preferred being proved an ingrate, idiot and all-around horse's ass to giving in. But these times were infrequent. I didn't particularly mind being an i., i. and h.a., but the process of establishing my status was just too damned wearying to be endured.

Pop spoke amusingly of "grown men, chasing a little white ball around a cow pasture." He looked down his nose as I boasted of "breaking forty." He himself had broken forty at my age, he said, forty acres of virgin land with only a one-horse plough.

I was spending two days a week at the golf course. Two days that once gone were lost to me forever. Two a week, one hundred and four a year—three hundred and twelve in three years.

Pop grew more eloquent with every word, and I grew older. When, at last, I retired to the bathroom for a smoke, it was with bent back and trembling, rheumatic legs. And I had to study myself in the mirror for minutes before I was convinced that I still had teeth and did not have a long gray beard.

Naturally, I retired from Glen Garden.

As I mentioned a while back, I had sold several short squibs to magazines. This activity was not encouraged, since my puny sales were taken as proof that I lacked talent and was frittering away my time, but neither was it actively discouraged. I had ceased to write, except occasionally and in the greatest secrecy, out of fear of publicity. I had taken a dreadful and prolonged razzing as the result of my writing, and I wanted no more of it.

Semaj Nosmot. How mellifluous the name had sounded when I invented it, and how hideous it became to me! Ah, vanity, vanity, what pitfalls dost thou mask. Semaj Nosmo . . .

I used that pen name only once, but unfortunately that once was on a return envelope. I returned home from school one evening to find myself addressed as Semaj and Nosmot, and I could see nothing at all funny about it—a fact which I was soon stating at the top of my lungs—but I was the only one who couldn't. Mom and Pop soon called a halt, seeing that I was badly hurt and upset, but they could not restrain an occasional snicker and chuckle, nor were they very successful in restraining Maxine and Freddie.

Wherever I went in the house there were whispers of "nosmot" and "snotpot" and "semaj" and "messy jam." And even as I started to flee the house, a chorus of catcalls drifted in from the street:

> Se-maj-uh Nos-mot
> Fell in uh pisspot

Maxine and Freddie had found the joke too good to keep. It had gotten into the public domain, all of which constituted enemy territory.

The above doggerel comprises but one of the jibes to which I was subjected in the ensuing weeks, and since there is no point in repeating it and the others are largely unprintable, I shall spare you further details of my ordeal. The point is that I had ceased to pursue writing for fear of being pursued by Nosmot.

But the furore had died down by now. The razzers had worn their material threadbare and were as weary of it as I was. It seemed safe enough to resume writing, but with the returns from magazines so small I tackled a new outlet. I gathered up the several invoices from my free-lance checks and exhibited them to the editor of the Fort Worth *Press*, modestly suggesting that in me there was at least the making of a star reporter.

He did not seem to look at me in quite that way. Or, for that matter, in any other way. With the ears beneath my pork-pie hat growing redder and redder, he remained bent over his work for the space of perhaps ten minutes. And he appeared deaf to the jovial patter which poured more and more desperately from my lips.

My skin-tight Valentino pants suddenly seemed six sizes too large for me. There was a terrible lump in the vicinity of my Adam's apple. Somehow, I gathered, I had erred grievously in my approach, but I could not think how it could have been. As a close student of Hollywood movies, I had become an expert on editor-reporter relations.

Reporters always sat down on the editor's desk. They always kept their hats on their heads, and cigarettes in their mouths. They always addressed the editor as "Old Socks" or "Kiddo" and tossed off such bright remarks as, "Don't pump me, Mac, I'm full of beer." I had done all these things. It looked to me like this guy didn't know his stuff.

At last, he looked up. Then he stood up. Silently, he plucked the hat from my head and the cigarette from my mouth. Then, he placed his palms against my shoulder and gently but firmly pushed me from his desk.

"Would you like to sit down?" he asked politely.

"Y-yes, sir," I stuttered.

"Please do," he said, gesturing to a chair.

I sank into it. He asked my age.

"Ffff-fourfifteen," I swallowed. "Almost fifteen."

"Oh?" His face softened. "I'd have said you were older. These checks—they're really yours? You've actually sold to those magazines?"

"Yes, sir."

"That's very good. I've never been able to sell as much as a two-line joke to a magazine. Why don't you just keep on with it? Why do you want a job on a newspaper?"

I explained the situation pretty incoherently, I imagine, but he seemed to understand.

"Well," he said, at last, "I can't offer you a thing. You go to school, you say, until three-thirty in the afternoon?"

"Yes, sir. But—"

"Can't offer you a thing. Nothing at all. Do you use a typewriter?"

"Yes, s—"

"Nope, it's out of the question. Nothing I can do for you. Know the city pretty well?"

"Y—"

"Well," he said casually, "I think we can probably work something out for you. But first—"

This was long before the founding of the American Newspaper Guild. Seasoned reporters drew twenty-five dollars and less for a work week of fifty and sixty hours, and youngsters breaking in frequently worked for no reward but the experience. So, for the times, the terms of my employment were more than generous.

I reported on the job at four in the afternoon (at eight A.M. on Saturdays), and remained as long as I was needed. For my principal duties as copy boy, phone-answerer, coffee-procurer and occasional typist, I was paid four dollars a week. For the unimportant stories I was allowed to cover, I was paid three dollars a column—to the extent that they were used in the paper.

Due to their very nature, my stories were usually left out of the paper or appeared in such boiled-down form that the cash rewards were infinitesimal. About all I could count on was my four dollars' salary—which just about paid my expenses.

This circumstance, coupled with the fact that I was away from home to all hours, soon resulted in a series of conferences between Pop and me. The discussions ended several months later when I ended my employment with the *Press*.

As is apparent, I was a very perverse young man. I customarily headed myself in exactly the opposite of the direction which others tried to head me, and I resented all attempts at reforming me. With this kind of make-up, I had profited about as little personally from my experience on the *Press* as I had in cash. But the seeds of improvement had been sown through the medium of example. I had been shown and allowed to observe, instead of being told. And gradually the seeds sprouted.

I abandoned my Valentino pants and haircut. I ceased to smoke except when I actually wanted a cigarette. I became careful about such things as shined shoes and clean fingernails. I started to become courteous. I was still guarded and terse, ever on the lookout for slights and insults, but I did not ordinarily go out of my way to be offensive. As long as I was treated properly—and my standards in this matter were high—I treated others properly.

I would like to say, in this connection, that good manners and consistent courtesy toward others are the most valuable assets a reporter can have. I know, having worked on metropolitan dailies in various of these United States. In my time, I have interviewed hundreds of people, notorious and notable. Movie stars and murders, railroad presidents and perjurers, princes, panderers, diplomats, demagogues, the judges and the judged. I have interviewed people who "never gave interviews," who "never saw reporters," who had "no statement for the press."

I once interviewed a West Coast industrialist, the third highest-salaried man in the United States. Because of his morbid fear of kidnappers he had made his home into a virtual fortress, and he was almost hysterical when I, having got hold of his phone number, called him up. He had never given an interview, he had never had his picture taken, and he would not do so now.

I told him I could understand his feelings and we would forget about the story. But would he be kind enough to talk to me for my own personal benefit? I had made no whopping success of my own life, I said, and I would appreciate a few pointers from a man who had. Grudgingly, and after checking back to see that the call was bona fide, he consented.

I went out to his house in the morning and I stayed on through lunch and into the afternoon. Finally, as I was getting ready to leave, he said that he felt rather uncomfortable about withholding the story. I said he didn't need to feel that way at all. I was in his debt for the privilege of talking to him.

"Oh, hell," he laughed abruptly. "I'm probably a damned fool, but—"

I got the story. Also a picture. Soon after that, since no one tried to rob or kidnap him, the industrialist got rid of his guards and his armament, and began enjoying life and his income.

Only once in my experience as a reporter did courtesy and consideration fail to pay off. That was in the case of a Washington real estate lobbyist, an ill-mannered boor with an inflated head whom all-wise Providence has since removed from circulation.

This man had sent advance notice of his arrival in the city where I was working, and I and the opposition reporters were at the train to meet him. We were there at his invitation, understand. But he looked through us coldly. If we wanted to talk to *him*, he said, we could do it at his hotel. We followed him there, and still he had "no time" for us. Perhaps, after he had had his breakfast.

We waited while he had his breakfast. We waited while he got his haircut. We waited while he kidded interminably with the cigar-stand girl. He then advised us that he was going up to his suite for a nap, and that he would "probably" be able to see us in an hour or so.

The other reporters and I looked at each other. We went to the house phones and conferred with our editors. Their opinion of this character happily coincided with ours—that he was a pea-brain who needed a lesson in manners, and that the pearls of wisdom which he allegedly had for our community should be retained for shoving purposes.

I relayed this message to the lobbyist. He slammed up the phone, threatening to get "all you bastards and your editors, too."

He got in touch with our publishers. He got in touch with our managing editors and our desk men. He threatened and blustered. He pleaded, he begged. He tried to bring outside influence to bear on the newspapers.

He called press conferences, and no reporters showed up.

He addressed banquets and meetings, and issued a steady stream of press releases. Not a word of what he said or wrote appeared in the newspapers.

Now, the real estate interests are probably the most powerful bloc in any community. But the potential club they formed, and which our friend had waxed vain in swinging, could swing more than one way. And so he soon found out.

The local realty operators began to look at him askance. What kind of man was it, they wondered, who could so mortally offend three large newspapers? In how many other cities had he incurred similar displeasure? They and other groups around the country were paying for his activities. They were paying him to influence legislation, to make them look good to the public. Was this the way he went about it?

The lobbyist was in complete disfavor with his nominal supporters when, at week's end, he sneaked out of town. But despite the all-around frost he had received, his manners remained virtually as bad as ever.

Back in Washington, he dished out considerably more boorishness than a certain party girl cared to take. She retaliated vigorously and effectively.

Her attack didn't quite kill him, more's the pity. But being concentrated on the area which the Marquis of Queensberry held sacrosanct, it did the next best thing.

Briefly, while the lobbyist may still be interested in women, he has nothing to interest them.

*Noblesse oblige!*

# XVI

AFTER LEAVING THE *Press*, I found brief employment on *Western World*, an oil and mining weekly. I had no regular hours, being summoned for work only during certain rush periods when extra help was needed. Neither did I have any regular duties. I did a little of everything, from addressing envelopes for the subscription department to reading copy to running errands to rewriting brief items. Occasionally, when there was space to fill, I also wrote poems —very bad ones, I fear—of the Robert Service type.

My pay was a magnificent three dollars a day, but I never knew when I would be called to work, having to hold myself in readiness at all times. And the times that I was called seemed constantly to conflict with my family's plans and schedules. Also, or so I imagined, my adult colleagues were not treating me with proper respect but consistently took advantage of their age and my youth to heap me with indignities.

They were all my bosses. All had the privilege of sending "Kid Shakespeare" and "young Pulitzer" after coffee or carbon paper, and they invariably chose to do so at the worst possible moments. As surely as there were visitors in the office, as surely as I was in the throes of epic composition, frowning importantly as I addressed my typewriter, there would be a cry of, "Hey, kid," followed by the suggestion that I wake up or get the lead out and busy myself with some quasi-humiliating errand or task.

This was probably all for my own good. A writer who cannot take it may as well forget about writing. But I had taken and was taking so much elsewhere, actually or in my imagination, that I could take little more. And finally, after a wild scene in which, to my horror, I very nearly bawled, I stormed out of the office and returned no more.

I went into a kind of decline during the next few months. I could not muster the slightest interest in the several part-time jobs I secured—in a grocery store, a bottling plant and on an ice wagon—and was soon severed from them. To all practical intents and purposes, I ceased to look for others. I was not unwilling to work, but I was not going to work for nothing—"nothing," being the standard rate of pay as I saw it. Moreover, I was not going to work at something that "didn't make any sense"—a category as generally standard as the rate of pay.

I played hooky more and more often, spending my school hours in burlesque houses. To finance these expeditions, I put in an occasional day at the golf course.

A photograph of this period reveals me as a thin, neat, solemn-faced young man, surprisingly innocuous-looking at first glance. It is only when you look more closely that you see the watchfully narrowed eyes, the stiffness of the lips, the expression that wavers cautiously between smile and frown. I looked like I hoped for the best, but expected the worst. I looked like I had done just about all I was going to do to get along and others had better start getting along with me.

I found people who met this last requirement at one of the smaller burlesque houses which soon received my entire patronage. It opened around ten in the morning, and except for interludes of cowboy pictures the stage shows were continuous. The performers saw me a dozen times a day, always applauding wildly. They began to wink at me, to nod, and soon we were greeting each other and exchanging brief pleasantries across the footlights.

There was an amplitude of seats during the hours of my attendance, so the manager-owner-bouncer made no objection to my semi-permanent occupancy of one of them. In fact, amiable man that he was, he came to profess pleasure over my patronage and alarm at my absences. He said he felt kind of funny opening the house without me, meanwhile sliding a pack of cigarettes into my pocket or asking if I'd had my coffee yet. He pressed me constantly to come clean with him, to tell him what I honestly thought of his shows. And he seemed never annoyed nor bored with my consistently favorable reviews.

I became a sort of fixture-without-folio around the place, showing up when I could, making myself useful when I chose. I relieved the ticket-taker. I butched Candy (Getcha Sweetie Sweets, gents—a be-ig prize in every package!). I assisted backstage with such widely assorted tasks as firing blank cartridges and hooking brassieres.

I drew no pay, but I was never in want. On the contrary, I ate and smoked much more amply than I had on my salaried jobs. The impression had become prevalent, somehow, that I needed looking after, and everyone took it upon himself to do so. Through the medium of the Friday "amateur shows" I was even provided with substantial amounts of spending money.

Perhaps you remember these shows, three-sided contests between the audience, the amateur and the implacable hook? Some totally talentless but determined wretch would stand stiffly center-stage reciting, say, Dan McGrew or singing Mother Machree. And the louder he talked or sang the louder became the howls and boos of the audience. He would persist, poor devil, even hurling back the squashy vegetables which were hurled at him. But his evil destiny would not be denied. The dreaded hook—a long pole with a shepherd's crook at the end—suddenly fastened around his neck, a stagehand yanked vigorously and the hapless amateur literally soared into the wings.

Lest nasty suspicions arise in the minds of the spectators, I could only appear on the show every two or three weeks. But I did very well at that, usually receiving the five-dollar grand prize, or at least the three-dollar second prize. And, yes, the judging was completely fair. My friend, the manager, held the various prizes over the various participants' heads. The amount of applause one received determined the size of his prize, if any.

I had a half-dozen very corny and completely unoriginal routines worked out with the assistance of the show's regular comics, but my act was usually confined to two which seemed to delight the audience more each time they saw them.

In one I dashed onto the stage with a prop bundle of newspapers under my arm, madly shouting such nonsense as "seven shot in a crap game," "ten found dead in a graveyard," "woman killed—Dick Ramsay's wife," "big disaster at soup factory—vegetables turnip and pea"—and so on for a matter of three or four minutes.

The second act, and the most popular of the two, was somewhat more elaborate. I strolled out of the wings, clad only in a lace baby cap and a diaper, and with a simulated chaw of tobacco in my cheek. Then, taking exaggerated aim at the props about the stage, I spat—the pit drummer providing suitable sound effects. And with every simulated expectoration a chair fell apart, a picture shattered, a milk bottle exploded or a table was shorn of a leg.

That was all there was to it, but the audience loved it. It was almost always the winner of the grand five-dollar prize.

One evening, following my act, when I was lounging backstage in my diaper, a man in puttees and a checkered coat suddenly appeared as from nowhere and virtually hurled himself upon me. I was, of course, guilty of all sorts of crimes, from truancy to smoking on street cars, and I was sure the total had long since equaled a capital offense. Thus I could only believe that this man was a detective and his rapid-fire babble an indictment. I neither heard what he said nor was able to reply. It was left to the performers to interpret to me and respond for me, which they repeatedly and enthusiastically did. But even after he had left, with a savagely jocular slap at my diaper, I remained in a trembling daze.

Me, an actor? A *motion picture* actor?

It just couldn't be.

It was, however, as I found out the following morning when I reported at what had been the office of a one-time lumber yard. The check-coated, putteed man was the director-producer of a brand-new picture company dedicated to the production of two-reel comedies. And I was to act in those comedies, starting as of right now. I had what it took, he assured me. ("Chaplin, kid, that son-of-a-bitch'll have to *swim* back to England.") He had been in the business for years and he was never wrong about these things.

I have since learned enough about picture-making to know that scenes are shot out of sequence, and they appear to be a meaningless jumble to one unfamiliar with the story involved. But knowing nothing of the kind, then, I became as bewildered as I was dazed. I moved in an all-too-apparent stupor, which no amount of shouting from the director-producer could snap me out of. My mind found much to feed its suspicion that I was the butt of a cruel joke.

In rapid order, I was costumed as a cowboy, a baker, a conductor (streetcar), a policeman, a lifeguard and a blind beggar. I was impelled to dive through windows, fall down steps and stumble into mud holes. I was knocked down, walked on, booted and tossed. I was hit with pies, crockery, salami, baseball bats and beer barrels. And once a live bull snake was hurled at me so that it twined around my neck.

The more I went through of this, the less I became accustomed to it. I performed like a zombie of the Piltdown era. Finally, his aggravation having increased by the fact that a blemish on my chin loomed monstrously large in the rushes, the director profanely discharged me.

I was one goddamned thing, he said, that he *had* been wrong about.

Naturally, having put him to so much trouble and expense, I received no pay.

The aforementioned blemish turned out to be the opening salvo in an attack of barber's itch, so for more than three weeks I was confined to the house, brooding over my recent failure and the many failures preceding it.

Actually, as I eventually learned, I had lost nothing. The picture company had begun operations on a shoestring, hoping to obtain financing via stockselling. Failing to do this, it had been unable to finish even that one first picture. It was never released, and the producer-director skipped town owing everyone.

I recovered from my malady and returned to the burlesque house. But I was no longer happy there as I had been. Everyone was nice to me, and everyone tactfully avoided the mention of motion pictures. Yet I was moody and restless. I felt that I had to do something—I simply *had* to. Something to rid me of the ugly stigmata of failure. Why, good God, I was almost sixteen years old and I had been a success at nothing!

Every night as I brooded wakefully in bed, I swore that I would make the following day different from the one just spent. But the following day found me spending it exactly as I had the previous one. I would be back at the burlesque house relieving the ticket-taker, butching candy, romping backstage with the chorus girls—wasting the golden hours which, once gone, would never come again.

Late one afternoon, a vaguely familiar-looking young man purchased a box of candy from me. He was both casual and brisk about it, first fumbling interminably for the necessary dime, then whipping out a five-dollar bill and impatiently demanding his change.

I counted it out to him. Just as I finished, his hand came out of the pocket with the dime he had been looking for.

"Here," he said, crisply. "Here's your dime. Let's have the five back."

I gave it to him—rather, I allowed him to withdraw it from my hand. I wandered absently on down the aisle, absorbed with the problem of doing *something*. And a full five minutes passed before it dawned on me that I had been done out of four dollars and ninety cents.

It was too late then, of course, to do anything about it. My fives artist would have skipped the show immediately and gone in quest of another sucker.

Nonetheless, I dashed back up the aisle looking for him. And there he was, still in the same seat, grinning at me and holding up the five.

"Just keeping in practice," he said, innocently. "You weren't worried, were you?"

# XVII

I HAD FIRST seen Allie Ivers in police court, where he appeared on a charge of swindling a storekeeper and I appeared in the interests of the Fort Worth *Press*. He was thin, blond and pale, with the most innocent blue eyes I have ever seen. He looked about sixteen years old the first time I saw him. He still looked sixteen, ten years later. Our paths crossed and recrossed during those years, and he often referred to me as his best friend (a reference which I often found debatable). I knew him far better than anyone else. Yet throughout our association, I never knew where he lived, I never learned anything about his background or antecedents, and I was never sure of how he would behave from one day to the next.

About all you could be sure of with Allie was that he would almost always do the unexpected—particularly if it was illegal—and to hell with the consequences.

Once, in an unusual moment of confidence, he gave me a hint of his philosophy. "I'd dive off a thousand-foot cliff," he said, "to get to a drowning man. After that, I don't know. Maybe I'd save him. Maybe I'd hang an anchor around his neck."

"First stealing his shirt," I suggested.

"Well," said Allie reasonably, "what would a drowning man need with a shirt?"

That was as close as I ever got to really knowing Allie. He remains the most imponderable of the strange characters who, throughout my life, have gravitated to me like filings to a magnet.

The judge took one look at him that day in police court and decided that no such demure youth could have "mitted" twenty dollars from the grocer's cash drawer, then short-changed him with his own money. He rebuked the arresting officer and dismissed Allie. I followed him outside.

Identifying myself as a reporter, I asked him to tell me the truth. Was he guilty or not?

Now, Allie's favorite reading was the penal code and his knowledge of law was something to turn a supreme-court justice green with envy. So, after a momentary start, he widened his wide blue eyes and confessed his guilt.

"That's not all," he said. "I stole a package of peanuts on my way out of the store."

I made a note of this, and Allie went on to recite other crimes. His regular occupation, he said, was stealing fur coats from whores. "They've all got them," he explained. "I don't know why they sock so much dough in coats when they spend nine-tenths of their time in bed."

I asked Allie about his *modus operandi*. He said it was simple. Having gained entry to the whore's room in the guise of a customer, he asked for a complete examination of the merchandise before purchasing. Then, with the deluded woman in the altogether and hence unable to pursue him, he grabbed her coat and fled.

"It's nice clean work," said Allie. "I'm going to get back to it as soon as the market gets better. Right now I've got all the pawnshops overstocked."

Allie said that next to stealing fur coats he liked to steal baggage. And this too was simple, he added modestly, involving little more than the ownership of a red cap and a badge. Also, he went on, he had done very well for himself by dividing the city into districts and assigning them to pickpockets on a percentage basis.

"My big trouble," said Allie, in conclusion, "is that I'm too restless. I keep jumping around from one racket to another. As soon as I get one going good, I move on to something else."

I was as preposterously naive in some ways as I was sophisticated in others. But I would like it made clear, lest I appear a bigger dunce than I was, that I believed Allie's story because it *was* true. Every word of it. This selfish young man had not only stripped whores of their hirsute habiliments and trusting travelers of their luggage, he had also defrauded some supposedly shrewd denizens of the underworld itself. In fact, as he confided to me later, he was never happier than when engaged in taking the takers. They put him on his mettle, added zest to existence in a way that the yokels never could.

In the case of the pickpockets, for example, Allie had visited Houston and Galveston, convincing a coterie of dips that the fix was in in Fort Worth and that, for a percentage of their take, he was prepared to assign them choice districts wherein they might "run wild." They fell for it—a number of them at least—and descended upon Fort Worth. Allie began collecting his percentage. The pickpockets began landing in jail.

To the run-of-the-mill operator, the incarceration of the

first pickpocket would have been a signal to skip town. But Allie Ivers definitely was not run-of-the-mill. As one after another of the pickpockets was knocked off, Allie went around to the others and explained that the guy had been gypping him on his percentage and had thus lost his license to steal. He sternly advised them to take heed and to make no errors in arithmetic while calculating his due. Understandably alarmed and anxious to retain his good will, the dips gave him his agreed on cut and more besides.

Within a very few days, of course, the true state of affairs became known, i.e., they had been paying for a fix which did not exist. But while there was an intensive search for him for a time, Allie also seemed not to exist. And the eventual opinion in police circles was that the pickpockets had created him, a fictitious fall guy, in the hope of excusing their own misdoings.

Allie spent the winter in Miami. "For my health," he explained, succinctly.

Well, though, to get back to the confession he had made to me, the truth or the falsity of it made not the slightest difference to a libel-conscious newspaper. True or false— and my editor called it a hop-dream on paper—it was a yarn such as to invite mayhem on the reporter who submitted it.

Being a man of exquisite courtesy and kindness, my editor merely folded and refolded it, forming it into a plug which he held in shape with a rubber band. He handed this to me.

"That hole in your head," he said. "Take care of it."

. . . Allie and I met outside the burlesque house, and he insisted on taking me to dinner. He said he had thought about me many times—worried about that story he had given me. He had meant no harm by it and hoped it had played no part in my descent to my present position.

I was pretty short with him, at first, but he seemed so

genuinely interested in my welfare that I swiftly thawed. We had dinner in a very good restaurant, and I brought him up-to-date on my activities. He laughed a great deal, but softly and sympathetically. There was the look in his eyes of a bored child who has stumbled upon a strange and intriguing toy.

"We'll have to do something about you," he kept saying. "Yes, we'll certainly have to do something."

"What kind of—uh—work are you doing now?" I asked.

"Bell-hopping," he said. "I'm down at the H—Hotel. It's not quite as good as stealing, but it's a change. I was getting pretty bored with the con."

"That's a pretty swell hotel," I said.

"I've been in worse," Allie shrugged. "They've got very good locks on the doors."

"Could I"—I hesitated—"Do you suppose I could—?"

"Why not? Why don't you ask?"

"Aw, I guess I better not," I said. "I have to go to school. I've been laying out a lot, but I have to go."

"That's all right," said Allie. "You can work at night. They have a hard time keeping boys on the night shift."

"I—I guess not," I said. "I—they wouldn't hire me. My folks wouldn't want me working at night, and—"

"Kind of lost your nerve, huh?" Allie nodded wisely. "Afraid to try anything for fear you won't make it. That won't do. Drink your coffee, and let's get going."

We went, with me lagging behind and protesting that I'd better not. At the side door of the hotel, Allie drew me up to the leaded panes and pointed to a paunchy, pompous-looking man with a carnation in the buttonhole of his black broadcloth coat.

"That's the man you see, the assistant manager on this shift," said Allie. "Now you go in there and tell him he either gives you a job or you'll piss in his hip pockets."

"Aw, for—" I tried to break loose.

"Do it your own way, then. I'm going to stand right here and watch you."

"Huh-uh, Allie," I muttered. "I don't look good enough, and—and I got a pain in my stomach, an' he'll think I'm crazy asking for a job in a place like—"

Allie's hand closed around my forearm in a grip that was surprisingly and painfully strong. "You get in there," he said, firmly. "If you don't, I'll yell for the cops. I'll say you made me an indecent proposal."

Something told me he would do exactly that.

I went in.

The assistant manager glanced at me wearily as I began a jumbled application for a job on nights. Then, while I was still mumbling he murmured a word which sounded like "hate" and which, I was sure, summarized his feelings about me, and strolled away.

Relieved that he had not had me arrested, I turned and tottered toward the door.

I had taken only a few steps when a swarthy, slick-haired young man with CAPTAIN emblazoned across his wine-colored jacket appeared at my side.

"You're going the wrong way, Mac," he said smoothly. "The tailor shop's back this way."

"T-tailor shop?" I said.

He grinned and took me by the elbow. "Couldn't understand Old Mushmouth, huh? You'll get used to him. Now, let's get you fixed up with a uniform."

# XVIII

I T WAS A weird, wild and wonderful world that I had walked into, the luxury hotel life of the Roaring Twenties. It was a world which typified rugged individualism at its best—or worst, a world whose urbane countenance revealed nothing of the seething and sinister turmoil of its innards, a world whose one rule was that you did nothing you could not get away with.

There was no pity in that world. The usual laws governing rewards and punishments did not obtain. It was not what you did that mattered, but how you did it.

Nominally, there were strictly enforced rules against such things as getting drunk on duty, intimacy with lady guests and forcing tips from the stingy. But the management could have knowledge that you were guilty of all those crimes, and as long as you did them in such a way as not to give rise to complaints or disturb the routine of the hotel, nothing would be done. Rather, you would be regarded as a boy who knew his way around and was on his toes.

And this attitude, I suppose, was not nearly so strange as it seems.

It was the bellboy who was always in closest contact with this hurly-burly world, a world always populated by strangers of unknown background and unpredictable behavior. Alone and on his own, with no one to turn to for advice or help, he had to please and appease those strangers: the eccentric, the belligerent, the morbidly depressed. He had to spot the potential suicide and soothe the fighting drunk and satisfy the whims of those who were determined not to be satisfied. And always, no matter how he felt, he had to do those things swiftly and unobtrusively.

Briefly, he had to be nervy and quick-thinking. He had to be adequate to any emergency. And a boy who was inadequate in his own emergencies was also apt to be so in those concerning the hotel. In a word, he wasn't "sharp." He didn't "know his way around," and thus, axiomatically, did not belong around.

In the indictments lodged against bellboys in the hotel "growler," the rough equivalent of a ship's log, one word appeared over and over—*caught*. A boy was fired or fined or turned over to the police because he had been *caught* in an offense, not merely because he had committed one.

There was no day off in the hotel world. The night shift worked seven days a week, from eleven at night until seven in the morning. The day shifts were also on the job seven days, but their hours were adjusted to the then universal long-day, short-day of the hotel world. One of the two shifts came on at seven in the morning, quit at noon, returned at six and worked until eleven at night. The following day it came to work at noon and quit at six P.M., the other shift working the double-watch long-day.

One night, when there was an unexpected flurry of business, a day boy was held over onto the night shift. It was his second holdover of the day, and he had been on duty since seven in the morning. So, after the business had been taken care of, he claimed the "late" boy's privilege of a room, and fell exhausted into bed.

Unfortunately, he had not rid himself of his cigarette before going to sleep. When he awakened a couple of hours later he was on the point of being incinerated and asphyxiated. Almost strangled, he got the windows open. Then he dragged the mattress and bedclothes into the bathroom and put them under the shower.

Scorched, but not seriously harmed, he got the fire out. But the expensive blankets, spread and box-mattress were ruined. Being caught in a mess like this would bring down the direst punishment which the hotel could devise.

The boy considered every angle of the seemingly hopeless situation. Then, he went downstairs, confessed his crime to the night clerk, and proposed a way of extricating himself with honor and profit. All he needed, he said, was the use of the emergency key (used in opening doors locked from the inside) and the assistance of one of the lobby porters.

Being exceeding sharp himself, the night clerk flatly refused. Under no circumstances would he involve himself in the matter.

"I'm going into the coffee shop for a bite to eat," he said. "And I had better not hear of you using the emergency key or the porters while I am gone."

"I understand," the boy nodded. "I see what you mean."

Now, one of the more or less regular residents of the hotel was a more-than-regular drinker, a man who passed out early and stayed passed out. It was his misfortune to be a guest of the hotel on this particular night.

He burst into consciousness from his stupor with his room filled with acrid fumes and his bed and himself literally floating in water. He did not need to ask the assembled company—which included the porter, clerk and bellboy—the cause of his plight. That was all too obvious. All he could do was thank them for saving his unworthy life, and offer recompense for the damage.

He tipped everyone handsomely. He distributed additional gratuities (without knowing it) when he paid the clerk's claim for damages. Then, because he had been so tractable in a trying situation, he was transferred to another room at no charge.

"It'll have to be one that's been slept in," the clerk explained. "But I know the former occupant quite well, and I assure you—"

"Not at all," the man protested. "Very kind of you."

So they took him down to the other room and put him to bed on a mattress and under bedclothes that were still warm with his own body.

News of this stunt spread throughout the hotel, and the employee participants were marked as men on their way up. As for their scapegoat, the management's attitude toward his part in the affair was also characteristic. Here was a man who got so besotted that he could be lifted and moved about without waking. Obviously, anyone who habitually attained such a condition was a menace to himself and the hotel.

So his name was entered on the "heel list"—a catalogue of undesirables—and he ceased to be a guest.

Since practically every hotel man worth his salt had begun his career as a bellhop, the tendency was not to be too severe on a sinner who, on the whole, appeared to be a "good boy." If you didn't "cry" (crying was bothering the management with a problem), if you were, by and large, personable, punctual and perspicacious, if you were an all-around boy—one who could fill in instantly for the valets, food checkers, waiter captains and the operators of elevators, switchboards and Elliott-Fisher machines—if you were all that, you were entitled to consideration no matter what your misdeed.

There was only one elevator operator on the night shift, and he was often too busy with guest traffic to bother with mere bellboys. Thus we were in the habit of opening up one of the driverless cars and transporting ourselves. This fact led to my first experience with the strange ways of hotel discipline, and a singularly terrifying experience it was.

I had been on the job about two months at the time, and was attending a party of vaudevillians in a third-floor suite. I had also been imbibing freely with those vaudevillians, so much so that I was very far from being sharp and on my toes. I left their rooms and trotted back to the elevator banks. I inserted a key in the door of my chosen car, swung the door open and stepped inside.

Inside the shaft, that is. Another boy had come along and taken my car.

I fell five floors in all—the three above-ground and an additional two into the basement and sub-basement. It wasn't an unchecked fall, of course. I was grabbing at cables and gear all the way. But you may take my word for it that even with full catch-as-catch-can privileges and no holds barred, a five-story fall is a hair-raising and painful ordeal.

I lay at the bottom of the pit for a few minutes, too shocked and pain-wracked to move. Then, groaning and mumbling dazedly, I sat up.

The pit door snapped open, and an ashen-faced engineer looked in at me. He helped me out, then ran to inform the room clerk of my accident.

This particular clerk—one of several I was to work with —was the epitome of all room clerks: crisp, cool and cynical. He looked me over, the corners of his mouth quirking strangely.

"Hurt pretty bad, eh?" he said. "Like to take the rest of the night off?"

"N-no, sir." I suppressed a groan. "I feel fine."

"You're drunk. You've got a breath that would knock a horse down."

"I haven't had a thing to drink," I said. "I've been chewing a new kind of cough drop."

"You're drunk. That's why you fell down the elevator shaft."

"Me?" I laughed shakily. "I didn't fall down the shaft, sir. I was—uh—"

"Go on. And you'd better make it good, understand?"

"I—uh—I save tinfoil, sir. Off of cigarette packages and gum wrappers. I climbed in there to look for some."

The engineer turned suddenly and departed. The clerk was abruptly stricken with a spasm of coughing.

He recovered from the fit, jerked out a pad of fine slips and began to write.

"You're going to have to sharpen up," he said curtly. "Get on your toes and stay there. You're a fairly good boy—show quite a lot of promise on some occasions—but you'll have to do a lot better."

"Yes, sir," I said.

"All right." He ripped off the fine slip and handed it to me. "Now get yourself washed up and cleaned up, and get up on that floor! Right away, understand?"

"Yes, sir," I said, and I looked down at what he had written:

> To J. Thompson, bellboy, $1 fine.
> Caught in general untidiness.

My next experience with the peculiar ways of hotel discipline came one morning when I had been held over onto the day shift. I was very tired and had taken a few drinks to pep myself up. Those few set so well with me that I took a few more, after which, as nearly as I could reconstruct events, I sat down in one of the lobby sand jars and went to sleep.

The bell captain promptly spotted me and I was hustled down to the locker room. The assistant manager, the same one who had hired me, followed us, vowing that I ought to be murdered.

"Of all the no-good blank blank blanks," he yelled, "you're the world's worst! You're fired, get me? Fired!"

"Y-yes, sir," I said.

"Another thing," he snarled, turning toward the door. "One more thing. Don't you dare come around here asking for your job back—for at least a week!"

To the best of my recollection, I was fired six times during my several years at the hotel. I was always rehired, sometimes within the same night. Five of my firings were for drinking, the other for smoking in a guest's room—all very serious offenses. Yet the hotel consistently rehired me where it curtly refused jobs to boys discharged for nominally trifling reasons. Failure, it seemed, could only be offset by ability. The "sharp" received every consideration, the dull got nothing.

This was all wrong, I am sure. But as a frequent traveler and diner-out, I often look back with longing on the days when an employee might be discharged on a moment's notice, without severance pay for himself or penalty for his employer—simply on the grounds that he was unsuited to his job.

# XIX

AS A BELLBOY I supposedly drew a salary of fifteen dollars a month, but in practice I seldom saw a penny of it. It was almost always consumed by fines, cleaning and pressing charges, insurance fees and the like. My earnings were in tips which ranged from virtually nothing a night to as much as fifty dollars.

On a bad night, a Sunday say, with no parties going on and few guests arriving, I might make less than a dollar. But on a good Saturday or during a lively convention, it would be no trick at all to knock off twenty-five, thirty-five or fifty or more dollars. Or, I should say, it was easy enough to do after I learned my way around. My first week on the job, I barely earned enough to pay for my cigarettes and carfare.

During normal times, only two bellboys were used on the night shift, and they were often idle except for the hotel's endless untipped "dead work." My first working companion, a "boy" of some forty years, took advantage of my ignorance to the end that I did the lion's share of the dead work and got a very small lamb's share of the profitable "bells."

He would take a call over the bell captain's telephone without letting on that it was a call. It would be a wrong number or a guest inquiring about his mail or something of the kind. Then, having saved up four or five bells, he would take care of them all on one trip. He also sent me on calls to empty rooms, and gave me bells which he knew to be trifling while he took the good ones.

After a week or so of this, I began to get wise to Pelly, or Pelican, as he was called, and I retaliated with the same stunts he had been pulling on me. I tried to reason with him. I pointed out that as surely as he tricked me, I would trick him and that we would both lose money as a result. But Pelican took this as a sign that I was weakening. He told me, in effect, to do my damnedest and that I would find his damnedest considerably better.

We night boys had many duties which took us behind the desk, chores such as cleaning the key rack and sorting mail. So, around three o'clock one morning, I removed a rate slip from the room rack and called Pell from a mezzanine house phone.

I spoke in a high, pseudo-feminine voice. I told him that the window in my room was stuck and asked for a bellboy's assistance in opening it.

Pell promised to take care of the matter, but I could tell he was suspicious. Peering through the rails of the mezzanine, I saw him hurry to the room rack, then nod triumphantly as he saw that there was no rate slip for the number I had given him. Obviously, or so he thought, the room was unrented. Actually, it was occupied by one of the crustiest old dowagers ever to curse a hotel with her patronage.

Pell snatched up the bell captain's phone and rang the room. I crept down the stairs, slipped around behind the key rack and returned the rate slip to its proper place. Then, I sauntered up behind him, listening to him read "me" off.

"I'm comin' after you," he was saying. "You keep up that squeaky-voice crap an' I'll come right up there'n get you. I'll turn you wrong side out. Kick your tail end right out through your teeth. Who I think I'm talkin' to? Why, you goofy pin-headed granny-dodger, I'm—I'm—"

He had turned and seen me. A look of pure horror spread over his face.

"Y-you," he stuttered, pointing a wobbling finger at me. "I th-thought that you—"

"Yeah?" I grinned at him. "As I was saying, Pell, I think we'd better stop rooking each other, don't you?"

He slammed up the receiver, silencing the outraged shrieks that were pouting over the wire. Lifting it again, he gave hasty instructions to the night switchboard operator. She was to say that the call had come in from the outside, from whom she did not know. If she made the story stick, he would buy her a five-pound box of candy.

Well, she made the story stick, and Pell escaped the penalty for his lack of sharpness. But never again did he gyp me on a call. We got along so well together that I felt quite depressed when he was literally chased out of the hotel. I was saddened by the event, but I still think it was one of the most hilarious I have ever witnessed.

Pell and the then room clerk, a Mr. Hebert, detested each other. Pell was constantly stating his intention of quitting or getting a transfer to days. Just as constantly, Hebert announced his intention to fire Pell or have him transferred. Yet neither did either. They chose rather to stay on the same shift, making things tough for each other.

Being in authority, Hebert would appear to have had the advantage of Pell. He could fine him, load him with dead work, bawl him out cruelly before other employees. Having done those things, however, and being unwilling to fire him, there was little else he could do. Pell, a mere bellboy with no authority, could do plenty.

He was a very smooth talker, a wonder at insinuating himself into the good graces of touchy and exacting guests. Having convinced such a person that he was "all for him" and hated to see him mistreated, Pell would reluctantly reveal that the man had been given the worst room in the house and at double the usual rate.

"They call this the dead room," he would say (to repeat one of his lies). "I think there must be some kind of germs in the wallpaper, the way everyone dies that stays here. Now, I know you won't let on that I told you—I just think you're a very nice gentleman, and I don't expect any big tip for tipping you off, but—"

At this juncture, the guest would usually tip Pell handsomely, step to the telephone and sulphurously demand that Hebert switch him to another room. Hebert would want to know why, naturally. The guest, enjoined to secrecy by Pell, would refuse to explain. He simply wanted another room, and he wanted it right now, by God, and he'd better not, by God, be gypped on the price.

Red-faced and bewildered, wondering, aloud, what the hell was getting into people, Hebert would do his best to satisfy the man. But the suspicions of a man who had been placed in the dreaded "dead room" at a double rate were not easy to assuage. By the time he had finished talking to the guest, Hebert was on the point of talking to himself. Sweat was pouring from his face and he was trembling in every joint, and there was a wild look in his eyes.

It was Pell who spread the rumor that Hebert wore no pants behind the high marble counter, a canard which—according to the sex and temperament of the guest—resulted in looks of disgust, scowls, and howls of laughter for the baffled and blushing room clerk. Pell was also responsible for the widespread belief that Hebert maintained a stable of whores in the hotel, renting them out at very low rates to gentlemen who could prove they were "all right."

"He don't care about the money, see," Pell would explain. "He's one of these guys that gets a bang out of it. Now, don't let on that I told you—"

Poor Hebert. He had a strong hunch that Pell was at the bottom of his many and maddening difficulties, but he could not prove it.

If Pell had had as much patience as ingenuity, I think he might have succeeded in his announced intention of driving Hebert nuts. But harassed as he was, Hebert stubbornly refused to crack up. And, annoyed by this perverseness, and emboldened by success, Pell attempted a master stroke.

As I have mentioned, there were two assistant managers. One was a primly urban man who managed to be both exquisitely efficient and completely unimpressive. The other, the "Mr. Mushmouth" who had hired me, was likewise an able hotel man but so turbulent and foible-filled that he seemed to mirror the strange world he worked in.

Essentially kindhearted, he was always a little wary, ready to leap down the throat of anyone who seemed to take advantage of him. Short and paunchy, he was also very vain— vain and sensitive. He was ever ready to interpret a friendly smile as condescension or a helpful gesture as a jibe. And hell had no fury like his when he felt himself slighted.

I got along very well with him, probably, I suppose, because we were much alike.

He would come in at the side door at around six in the morning of his long day, his shoulders hunched like a prize fighter's, his sleep-haggard face set in a deep and watchful scowl. Crossing the lobby at a steady but wary gait, he would pause at the end of the long marble counter, where he liked to find me stationed, and slowly turn sideways to it. Then, he would remove his beautiful Homburg hat and diffidently thrust it at me.

"Mrningjim," he would grunt.

"Mrningsir," I grunted back at him.

"Srningouside."

"Rnedallnightsir."

"Huh."

"Yuhsr."

At this point he would usually turn and scowl at me and I would scowl back at him. But sometimes, when the feeling was upon him, he would continue the "conversation" for several minutes, deliberately speaking with increasing unintelligibility and being replied to similarly, until we made less than no sense at all.

I was the only one he would speak to until he had had his breakfast. Hebert, poor soul, insisted on crying out a cheery "good morning" to him, but all he got in return was a hate-filled glare.

After breakfast, the assistant manager would return to the lobby for a brief report on the night's events from Hebert. Then, he would reclaim his hat and make an outside inspection of the hotel. His routine was always the same. He was always the same. Vain, sensitive, quick tempered. Thus, the raw material of Pell's plot against Hebert.

There was a great deal of paper work on the night shift, and Hebert was supplied with a rubber stamp of his name to use on the countless invoices and charge slips which required his endorsement. Pell obtained an impression of the stamp on a piece of paper. He had a duplicate made and brought it to work with him. Then . . .

The explosive and suspicious little assistant manager was in an even more terrible mood than usual that morning. He barely grunted at me, and he looked like he could have killed Hebert for the latter's insistently cheerful greeting. Shoulders hunched, hands clenched into fists, he disappeared into the coffee shop.

Pell plucked the Homburg from my fingers, and went behind the keyrack. I followed him immediately, but he had already begun his vandalism and nothing was to be gained by interfering with him. I could only stand and watch as, over and over, until the fine silk lining was a mess, he stamped the name *E. J. HEBERT* in the assistant manager's hat.

"Now," he said, "you and I had better get out of here. We don't want to be around when Old Mushmouth comes after his lid."

"You're telling *me*," I said.

We hid on the mezzanine directly above the cashier's cage where Hebert was working. We waited, listening to the occasional thud as Hebert used his stamp. The assistant manager returned and they conversed briefly. Then, seeing that neither Pell nor I were around, the A.M. asked Hebert to hand him his hat.

"Certainly, sir," said Hebert. And, still carrying his rubber stamp, he went around behind the key rack.

Pell and I returned to the lobby, he by the front stairs, me by the rear. I made myself as inconspicuous as possible, but Pell took up a position on front post, only inches away from the window where the assistant manager was waiting.

Hebert came back with the hat, carrying it tenderly crown-up as he had found it. He passed it through the window.

"Ankyou," grunted the assistant manager, starting to lift it to his head. Then, he paused, eyes popping, and said, "Wottnell!" He looked up, glaring terribly at Hebert, and an almost subhuman growl came from his throat.

Hebert smiled nervously. "Something wrong?" he said.

The assistant manager made no answer. He simply grabbed Hebert by the necktie, hauled him halfway through the window and began beating him with the hat.

The room clerk was taken completely by surprise, but he was not too dazed to see that Pell had somehow inspired the assistant manager's attack. So he grabbed the bellboy by the collar and dragged him into the fray. For every blow he received he gave one to Pell, and Pell, tangled between the two men and helpless with laughter, was powerless to resist.

The assistant manager tried to shove him out of the way, the better to get at Hebert. But the clerk hung onto him. Pell was jerked back and forth, catching the blows intended for Hebert as well as those intended for him. And as the struggle waxed furious, an ink pad flew from his pockets and a rubber stamp with it.

Panting, the assistant manager released his hold on Hebert and made a grab for Pell. "Bstd!" he snarled, flinging himself at the bellboy. But fast as he was, he wasn't quite fast enough.

The last I saw of Pell he was heading for the rear landing, and the assistant manager was right behind him, aiming a kick at his fleeing posterior at every third step.

# XX

A FEW YEARS ago I met one of the boys—by then a
man, of course—I formerly hopped bells with. He
was the owner of an automobile agency in a large
southwestern city, and I also was enjoying some small success. Naturally, we fell to discussing the other boys we had
known, those whose later lives were familiar to us.

One had been killed by the FBI while resisting arrest as a
suspected kidnapper. One had been hopelessly crippled
while attempting to blow up a safe. Two had committed
suicide when still very young men. One had overdosed himself with salvarsan, bit his tongue off in a spasm of agony
and drowned in his own blood.

Not a very pretty picture, but that was only part of it.
Another boy of our acquaintance had become a renowned
geologist, another a doctor and another a minister. Two
others were managers of large hotels.

"All in all," my friend said, "I suppose about as many of us turned out all right as didn't. About the same percentage you'd find in any other group."

"That's true," I nodded, "the percentage is the same. But I don't think you'll find the division within another group so drastic. Take a bunch of grocery clerks starting out together, or a group of filing clerks or service station attendants. Some will get ahead, some won't. But the spread between them won't be small and gradual. Five of them will die violent deaths while the other five become relative big shots."

My friend frowned, thoughtfully. "Y'know," he hesitated, "it's kind of like it was on the job, isn't it? There wasn't any middle ground. You were either in or you were out."

"That's the way it looks. It did you a lot of good or a lot of harm."

"Which do you think it did you?"

"Well," I said, "I'm here."

In most pursuits, temptation stands on the sidelines. It does not grab but beckons, and once passed it is gone. But it was not thus in the luxury hotel of my day. Temptation followed you, placing herself in your path at every turn. And, paradoxically, succumbing to her often meant a reward, and resistance, punishment.

You worked in the hotel, but you worked for the guests. Your earnings, your very job depended upon their good will. So why offend a wealthy drunk by refusing to drink with him? Why snub a lovely and well-heeled widow when it was so easy to please her? And what about these people, anyway? If they were all wrong—these publicly acclaimed models of success and deportment—then who was right?

There was an unhealthy tendency to acquire complete contempt for the monied and a consuming regard for money. Money was apt to mean far too much and people nothing.

Living in a world of topsy-turvy standards and constant temptation, a boy could easily become involved in serious and long-lasting trouble. To survive in that world he had to be very, very lucky and have a fair degree of intelligence. But more than anything else, he had to be able to "take it," to absorb the not-to-be-avoided abnormal without being absorbed by it. Or, to state the matter simply, he needed a strong sense of humor.

If he had that, he was usually all right. Far from harming him, the hotel life would do him a lot of good.

It was during the big conventions of business and fraternal organizations that, as the saying was, the men were separated from the boys. They descended upon the hotel on an average of twice a month, and I grew to look upon them with a kind of delighted horror. They meant much money, but they also meant wracked nerves and utter physical exhaustion. All the incongruities and inconsistencies of hotel life were multiplied a dozen times over.

A day or so before a convention started, the hot-shots would drift into town. These were the professional bellboys —men—who traveled the country over and made a career of working the conventions. They knew all the angles and they played them all. They had to.

All bellboys paid a daily "tax" or "kick" to the captains for the privilege of working. The convention hot-shots not only paid this, but they also paid for their jobs. During an oil men's convention, for example, a four-day job sold for two hundred dollars plus a daily tax of ten dollars.

Since selling jobs is a federal offense, the question of what happened to all this money is one I consider too delicate to answer. But I will say that no hot-shot ever successfully appealed a bell captain's decision to the management. And one of the captains told me he was "goddamned lucky to hang onto a third of the take."

The hot-shots received nothing for their money but the hotel's permission to go to work. There was no guarantee that they would not be fired or jailed thirty minutes after they stepped on the floor. There was no guarantee that they would be able to get—or hold onto—a uniform to work in. That was their headache, something to be worked out between them and the regular bellboys.

There were never more than twenty-five uniforms—but the number of bellboys during a convention often rose to a total of forty. And while the hot-shots were tough, the regulars were no pantywaists. So every change of shift marked the beginning of a battle with as many as three boys struggling for the same uniform.

Lockers were broken into. Tailor shop employees were threatened and bribed. Boys were tripped up and knocked down and sat on and stripped of their uniforms. One did not enter the locker room unless he was prepared to do battle.

Not all the quarrels arose over uniforms. Gypping on bells was the order of the day, and if a guy didn't like it he knew what he could do about it.

Those fights. They were strange, hideously fascinating affairs.

The combatants-to-be would first remove their uniforms and stow them away for safekeeping. Then, wordlessly and without preliminary, the fight would start. Its one rule was that no blows could be struck to the face. A knee in the groin was all right. A kick in the instep was all right, or a rupturing punch to the kidneys or a paralyzing blow to the heart. But a man's face must never be marked.

The fighters would weave their way through the crowded locker room, here passing in front of a boy who was shaving, there squeezing between a pair who were fastening one another's collars. No one paid any attention to them. No one tried to interfere. Everyone had more than enough to do to take care of himself.

Since all the boys were above average toughness and since one rarely knew a dirty trick unknown to the other, the fights usually ended in some kind of compromise. A no-gyp compact would be sworn to or an agreement would be arrived at whereby a uniform and a working-shift were shared. Often it was that way, but not always. Inevitably, some of the hot-shots were driven on and some of the regulars driven out.

Everyone had it in for everyone else. No matter what he made, no one was satisfied. There were thousands of dollars in cash among the bellboys as the end of a convention approached, and every boy knew it and wanted it. Not just part, but all. This resulted in twenty-four-hour-a-day dice games in the locker room. Some of the biggest games I have ever seen, and I have seen some big ones.

The play would go on and on, with the players dropping out when they lost the dice, hopping bells for an hour or so, then getting back into the game as their turn came again. It was an all-or-nothing contest. No man was allowed to quit winner as long as the others wanted to play. If one was forced to drop out of the game, his winnings were impounded with one of the captains.

They could be maddening things, those "last man takes all" games. With forty boys involved, the odds were forty to one against your being the final victor. Yet I could never keep my money in my pocket where it belonged.

I would come down at night, and lay bets while I dressed. I might be cleaned out immediately, but more often than not I would win. Five hundred, a thousand, fourteen or fifteen hundred. But always the time came when I had to quit— leaving my winnings with the captain. (The captains, I should say, were well-chaperoned during their comings and goings.)

When the end of the convention came, and the final game with it, I sometimes had two or three thousand dollars "riding." And I would envision myself as that lucky last boy, a teenager retired on a modest fortune. Now, however, "piker bets" were disallowed. You faded what the other man wanted to shoot—and what he often chose to shoot was the exact amount of your winnings. The others had come into the game with big bankrolls and added to them. They could double up and triple up on the bets, cleaning you—or I should say, me—out in minutes. And, needless to say, they invariably did.

Still and all, thanks to a confidential talk with Allie Ivers, I did not do too badly in these games. I never got out with my temporarily won thousands. But by the process of "rat-holing"—surreptitiously palming an occasional ten or twenty—I often got away with hundreds.

The cops on the beat were aware of these dice games and frequently came in for a few minutes to watch the play. On the whole, they were like most of the other cops I have known—good, honest fellows doing a hard and thankless job at low pay. But there was an exception in the person of a cop called Red, a husky giant with close-set eyes who had admittedly donned a shield for what he could get out of it.

Red was always gambling and losing, then lying about the sum he had lost and grumbling that the game was crooked. He was always begging for a few dollars to get back into the game—the loan being repayable on a tomorrow that never arrived. The boys sneered at him, insulted him, profanely refused to fade when he was shooting. Still Red hung on, a whining, grumbling, insult-proof sponge.

I had been bell-hopping for something more than a year when Red tried to tap me for ten dollars. I told him to go to hell. More accurately, I told him I wouldn't lend him the sweat from my socks if he paid me Niagara Falls for inter-est.

"Why, Jesus Christ!" I protested, my voice cracking with irritation. "What's the matter with you, anyway? You're a cop—you're supposed to be someone. How in hell can you hang around here begging money from bellboys?"

"Aw, come on," he insisted, not in the least embarrassed. "What's ten bucks to you? You've got plenty of dough."

"Nothing doing," I said. "You've already four-bitted me out of five or six bucks. Chisel someone else."

"I'll pay it back. First thing tomorrow."

"Nuts."

I went on dressing, trying to ignore him, but he wouldn't give up. He didn't want the money to shoot craps with, he said. He didn't even want it for himself. He needed it for his wife and baby, for some medicine and groceries.

"Wife and baby?" I said. "I didn't know you were married."

"Sure, I am. Been married right along. Come on, Jimmie. I wouldn't ask you for it if I just didn't have to have it."

"Well," I hesitated, "I've got a family of my own to take care of. If I was sure you'd pay the dough back—"

"Tell you what I'll do," he said promptly. "I'll hock my night stick with you. That's good security. You know I can't get by working very long without it."

"All right," I said. "I think I'm making a mistake, but—"

I gave him the ten and locked his night stick in my locker.

When I came to work the following night, the locker had been broken open and the club was gone.

I was pretty sore, to put it mildly. But the situation appeared to have its bright side. Having done this to me, Red would doubtless steer clear of the hotel for some time to come.

I was starting to change clothes, consoling myself with the thought of Red-free nights sans whining and begging, when the locker-room door opened and in he came. He was grinning broadly. The night stick was dangling from his wrist.

"About that club," he said. "A fellow over at the station house had an extra he wasn't usin'. He gave it to me."

"I see," I said.

"So I guess I'll just let you keep that other one."

"All right," I said.

"You don't mind, do you?" he grinned. "That's all right with you, ain't it?"

"Supposing it wasn't?" I said.

"Yeah?" He chuckled. "Supposin'?"

He went out, laughing openly. I went on dressing. I'd paid ten bucks to get the horse laugh, and I had to like it. I'd been dared not to like it.

Allie Ivers had come onto the night shift with me and knew of my loan to Red. He was as chagrined as I when I told him how Red had repaid the favor.

"You're not going to let him get away with it, are you?" he demanded. "Don't tell me you're just going to grin and take it!"

"What else can I do?"

"Fix the bastard's clock! Make him wish he'd never been born!"

"Yeah? And how am I going to do it?"

"I'll think of something," Allie promised.

He did think of something, and before the night was over. I listened to his scheme incredulously, by no means sure that he wasn't joking.

"You're kidding." I forced a laugh. "We can't do anything like that."

"Sure, we can," said Allie. "I'll get this babe I know to give him a fast play, make a date with him. She'll give him the number of one of the rooms the hotel's blocked off for the summer. When he comes in here—you'll have to slip him upstairs, of course—I'll—"

"But a—a *cop!*" I protested. "My God, Allie—to do that to a cop!"

"He's no cop. Wearing a uniform doesn't make a man a cop. What's the matter with you, anyway? I'm trying to do you a favor."

"Well, I—"

"I thought you trusted me."

"Well, I—"

I was still less than seventeen years old. And seventeen is seventeen, no matter what it has been through or up against. Moreover, despite my patent hardheadedness, I suffered from a deeply rooted feeling of inferiority. I wanted to be liked, and felt impelled to defer to those who gave me liking.

So I consented to Allie's plan. Two days later, at about two-thirty in the morning, Red beckoned to me furtively from the lobby side entrance.

I went out to the walk. He pressed a ten-dollar bill into my hand.

"Just playing a little joke on you," he said, giving me an amiable nudge in the ribs. "Okay? We're friends again?"

"What do you want?" I said.

He told me—although, of course, I already knew. Suddenly, as though it were another's voice speaking, I heard myself refusing.

"You've got no business up there. No one's got any business there. Those rooms are blocked off. They're too hot to stay in this time of year. Why, they haven't even got any bedding in 'em, and the telephones are discon—"

"Oh, yeah?" He grabbed me roughly by the arm. "Don't hand me that stuff! I got plenty of drag around this town. You try to crap me, an' I'll make you hard to catch."

"All right," I said. "If that's the way you want it."

He went around to the rear entrance, and I took him upstairs on the service elevator. He followed me down to the hall to a small court room. Then, dismissing me with a contemptuous nod, he tapped on the door. It opened, and he stepped into the darkness.

There was a dull thud and a grunt, and the door closed again.

I went back to the rear landing where I waited nervously for Allie. He arrived shortly with Red's pants which he tossed down the incinerator chute. He similarly disposed of the key to the room.

"Everything's fine," he assured me, urging me toward the elevator. "Didn't hurt him a bit."

"But Allie, I—what's going to happen to him?"

"How do I know?" said Allie, cheerfully. "I'd say he'd probably sweat to death if he stays in that room very long. Good riddance, too."

"But—"

"Yes, sir," Allie mused, "it's quite a problem all right. He can't call for help. He can't use the telephone. And if he did manage to get down the fire escape, where would he go from there? What's he going to do without—"

"Allie," I said, "I just remembered something. They've got the water cut off in those rooms. We can't leave him there in this weather without any water."

"He's got plenty," said Allie. "I noticed there was quite a bit in the toilet bowl."

Whatever Red's sufferings were, during the two days he spent in that room, they could have been as nothing compared to mine. I was sick with fear and worry. Finally, on the night of the second day, I insisted on putting an end to Red's imprisonment.

Allie pointed out that Red could gain release from the room any time he chose to. All he had to do was pound on the door until someone heard him.

"But he can't do that! How would he explain—"

"I wonder," said Allie.

He was entirely prepared to leave Red in the room until thirst and heat and hunger drove him to some act of desperation. But seeing that I was on the point of a nervous collapse, he reluctantly gave in to me.

We filched the passkey from the desk, and a pair of

porter's pants from the laundry. Early the next morning, some two hours before the end of our shift, we went up to the room.

The door was still locked from the outside. We unlocked it cautiously, looked in and went in.

Red was gone.

Obviously, he had left by the fire escape. But what he did after reaching it, I do not know. He may have crept down to the alley at night and hailed a cab. Or he may have gone up the escape to another room, helped himself to the occupant's clothes and then made his exit. I don't know how he got away from the hotel. Only that he did.

Allie and I learned that he had been fired from the force, presumably for absence without leave. Yet the grins and winks of the other cops hinted that this was not the sole reason for his dismissal. Apparently and literally, Red had been caught without his pants. As a result of this, we gathered, he had not only been fired but also "floated" out of town.

"Like a bum," said Allie. "And what's wrong with that?"

# XXI

PA—MY GRANDFATHER—used to say that being broke wasn't so bad, but going broke was pure hell. Watching Pop's decline, his brief and occasional ups and his long steady downs, I saw the bitter wisdom of Pa's philosophy.

Having drilled four dry wells for himself, Pop began drilling on contract for others, mortgaging his oil field equipment to get the necessary financing. He did very well on the first contract, and almost as well on the second. But the third was a financial failure plus. The drill bit struck granite a few hundred feet down, and this virtually impenetrable rock forced him to take a year to drill a well which should have been completed in a month. He lost all of his earlier profits and all of his drilling equipment and wound up thousands of dollars in debt.

Our cars were sold, our house and furniture mortgaged. He leased a smaller rig, and went into the business of pulling pipe from abandoned wells. But the cycle of mild successes and whopping failures still pursued him. Two jobs made money, the third was a break-even, the fourth put him out of business, his credit ruined and more deeply in debt than ever.

He set himself up as a rig (derrick) building contractor— an enterprise which required only hand tools and labor. And here at last, it seemed, he was on his way back up. He squeezed the last possible penny from every contract. He oversaw his own jobs. He did hard physical labor himself.

But he was getting old, nearing an age when active participation in an exacting business would be impractical. And while he made some money on every job, it was never very much. With little but his time and experience to invest, his income was proportionate. To get into the big money you had to take turnkey contracts—i.e., you supplied all necessary material for a job, as well as the labor. By so doing you profited on dozens of commodities, instead of one, and your overall reward was large, if, of course, you figured correctly and nothing went wrong.

So Pop sunk everything he had and everything he could get into a turnkey contract. And his estimates were so sound that he completed it days ahead of the penalty date. He sent due notice to the contractee. The latter wired his congratulations. He would arrive the following day to inspect and accept the job.

Well, he arrived all right. But by the following day, there was no job to inspect. The first tornado in its history had struck the area. Splintered to smithereens, the rig was scattered over half the county.

With no capital and no credit, Pop became a dealer in leases, or, to use a contemporary and contemptuous term, a lease louse. There were thousands like him in the oil country cities. Middlemen of middlemen—men so far removed from the principals in a deal that they frequently did not know the latters' identities.

One would get hold of a lease on a short-term option. Another would assume the job of getting it drilled (necessary to validation) on a percentage basis. He had no assets of his own, but he knew someone who knew someone with assets, supposedly. And this last person knew someone who knew someone who would do the drilling for part cash and an interest. And the part-cash man knew someone who knew someone who could get workmen on a cash-interest basis. And—

But enough. It was not as funny as it may sound.

Sometimes, at the end of a transaction, there were a few thousands to split up between the dozens of "lice." Rarely, however, was a transaction carried through to a successful culmination. Somewhere along the way, as it moved from one broke broker to another with each snipping away a fragment, it simply disappeared.

One of the choice jokes around Fort Worth concerned a "louse" who turned out to be a dozen other guys. He put a short-time option into the mill. Then, knowing the ramifications through which it must proceed, plunged back into the milieu of someone who knew someone. After weeks of frantic effort the first deal seemed ready to bear fruit. All the principals and sub-principals and sub-sub-principals were to meet in his office. As he waited for them, his one worry was that they might not all be able to crowd into the tiny cubbyhole.

The time of the meeting came and went. Hours passed and it grew dark, and still the louse remained alone. Finally, the tragicomic trugh dawned on him. No one was going to show up, because "everyone" was already there.

I could never laugh much over that joke, since Pop was the louse involved. He gave up his cubbyhole and became a curbstone operator. I looked him up one morning and asked him to come to breakfast with me.

He did so, rather coolly. He had been cool and formal with me for some time. At first he had argued sternly against my going to work at the hotel. Then, his affairs went from bad to worse, and my earnings were necessary for the maintenance of the family. Pop's attitude changed. He no longer argued.

It seemed to him, I suppose, that I had usurped his position in the family. I could not help it, perhaps, nor could he, but the fact remained. I was my own man. So be it.

We were like polite strangers to one another, rather than father and son.

So, this morning, we sat across from each other in the restaurant booth, dabbling aimlessly with our food and talking in monosyllables. And, finally, after a number of false starts, I managed to broach the subject that was on my mind.

"It's about one of the guests at the hotel, Pop. He's acted kind of funny ever since he checked in. Always watching me when he thought I wasn't looking, and making up excuses to talk to me. Prying into my background. Well, last night I took some cigarettes up to his room, and he opened up with me. I found out what it was all about."

"I see," Pop murmured absently. "Very interesting."

"Well," I hesitated. "The point I'm getting at—what I wanted to ask you was, did you ever hear of a man named L——?"

"L——?" Pop showed a little more interest. "I knew him fairly well. He was on President Harding's private train with me for a day and a night."

"What became of him?"

"No one knows. He was president of some corporation in Kansas City. He disappeared one night with more than a million and a half dollars of the company's assets—cash and negotiable securities. Why do you—?"

Pop broke off abruptly, his eyes suddenly sharp with interest. I nodded.

"He's here, Pop. It's the same guy I was telling you about. He's still got most of the loot, and he'll give it up if he's promised immunity from prosecution. He trusts you, more than he trusts anyone else, anyway. Can you swing it? I mean can you—c-can we make the bonding company give us a cut for—?"

I was afraid he'd say no, he was always so straitlaced and upright about everything. But he had been a lawyer and knew that such deals were made every day. The proposed transaction was entirely legitimate, he said, and he became almost as excited over it as I was.

"What's his room number? I'll call him right now, and tell him—"

"He's checked out," I said. "He moved out of the hotel as soon as he'd talked to me, and I don't know where he went to. But we made arrangements for us to meet him tonight. How much would we make on the deal, Pop? Five or ten thousand?"

Pop laughed fondly. "Somewhat more than that," he said. "Ten per cent is the usual fee for a negotiator, and I imagine the bonding company would be very happy to pay it. In other words, if L——has as much as a million and a half left, we should get—"

"A hundred and fifty grand? Wow!"

We talked and talked, becoming really friendly for the first time in months. I confessed that along with being pretty stubborn and hard to handle I had been drinking far too much—that anything at all was too much for a boy my age. Pop confessed that his own behavior left much to be desired, and declared he was turning over a new leaf. Things would be different with us from now on. He'd get into some safe but reasonably profitable branch of the oil business. I'd quit the hotel and concentrate on school—get out of high school some way, and go on to college.

Pop and I agreed that it was best to say nothing to Mom about the impending deal. Not too worldly wise, it would only worry her.

We ran through the arrangements for meeting that night, making sure we had them right. Then, since it was far too late for me to go to school, I went on home.

Mom was pretty cranky with me. Unlike Pop, she did not feel that my financial contributions to the family exempted me from parental dominion. She wanted to know why I hadn't gone to school instead of "loafing around town." And she obviously did not at all care for the evasive answers I gave her.

She scolded and fussed, until at last there was nothing left to say and she was as weary as I. I went to bed, then, telling her to call me at seven as I wished to see a show before going to work.

I was supposed to meet L——at eight-thirty on the bridge over the North Trinity River. He would pick me up in a car, providing I was alone and he deemed it safe, and we would drive on into the packing-town section of Fort Worth. At nine-thirty, still providing that L——was given no cause for alarm, we would pick Pop up in an isolated area. They would then exchange commitments, as attorney and client, and the details of the transaction would be worked out.

Well, Mom did not call me at seven, but at nine. She said that if I was too tired to go to school, I was too tired to go to shows. It was ten o'clock before I got to the bridge, an hour and a half late for my appointment with the suspicious, badly frightened L——.

It was too late, of course. I waited for him until it was almost one, making myself seriously late for work, but he never showed up. Where he went to or what became of him, I do not know.

I was sick with disappointment, and the blow was a crushing one for Pop. As for Mom, well, what was the use in telling her the truth—that the two hours of sleep she had forced on me had cost more than one thousand dollars a minute?

# XXII

O N WEEK DAYS I went from work to school and remained in class until three-thirty in the afternoon. It
was usually five or six o'clock before I could get to
bed, and I had to rise at nine-thirty in order to be at work on
time. Obviously, I did not get much sleep. Daytime sleep is
apt to be an uneasy thing, achieved in spats and spurts which
leave one wakeful but unrested. Frequently, during the daz-
zlingly hot Texas summer, I went whole days with no sleep
at all.

Being of very hardy stock, I seemed little affected by my
rigorous near-sleepless life for more than two years. But it
was telling on me. I had acquired a persistent and annoying
cough. My appetite was almost nonexistent. I was drinking
more and more, so much so that I was buying pints and
quarts instead of depending on free drinks from guests.

Also, although the fact was hard to detect on one with my wiry build, I was losing weight steadily.

As I passed my eighteenth birthday and entered my third year at the hotel, the hitherto concealed signs of illness began to break through to the surface. I was suddenly gaunt instead of merely thin. I had brief but frightening spasms of nervous trembling. My cough had a hollow echoing sound. I was filled with morbid self-doubts, and no amount of whiskey would completely dispel them.

Mom and Pop begged me to quit the job. In our circumstances, the suggestion seemed maddeningly foolish and I refused to discuss it.

Because I was supposed to be a "fairly good boy," the nominally hard-boiled management tried to give me a hand. The word filtered down from somewhere that I should not be fined or disciplined except on higher authority, and I should not be held over except in extreme emergencies. Moreover, if I chose to sleep an hour or so at night in one of the checked-out rooms, no one was to take notice of it. And whatever I wanted to eat within reason was to be provided at no charge by the coffee shop chefs.

I appreciated these favors, both for their intrinsic value and for the good will they reflected. But I enjoyed them no more than a week or two before I was forced to call a halt. They made the other boys too resentful. A man may survive with the disesteem of his employers, but let him be generally disliked by his fellow-workers and he is through.

My friend the assistant manager, he of the sensitive soul and the terrible temper, had shown increasing concern for my obvious illness. He always lingered for a few moments after handing me his hat, mumbling diffident inquiries as to how I was getting along and grumbling suggestion to take it easy.

"Better get off of bells," he suggested one morning. "Try you on something else."

And try me he did.

In succession, I worked as assistant night auditor, valet, food checker, telephone operator, elevator operator, steam presser and assistant maître d'hôtel. But in the end I came back to bell-hopping.

I believe that the challenge of so many jobs was good for me, and I certainly acquired much valuable experience. But I was not improved healthwise, and I could not afford the financial loss which the other positions put me to. They paid well enough, I suppose, but the amounts seemed niggardly compared with my bellboy earnings. So, half regretfully, I returned to my original job.

I dragged through the months, obsessed with a weird feeling that I was slowly falling apart. And though I felt pretty hopeless about it, I attended school faithfully. This was my last chance, I knew—the last year I would be going to school. Either I got out now, with proper scholastic credit, or I never would. My six years of misery and frustration there would be wasted.

Spring came, and suddenly I felt better than I ever had. I was eating and sleeping less than ever, coughing harder and drinking more. But still I felt wonderful. Nothing seemed to bother me. I was never tired, my mind had never been sharper. I was brimming over with good feeling, always smiling, always ready to burst into laughter at the smallest joke.

My extensive reading had not carried me into the fields of psychiatry and morbid psychology; hence, I accepted my feeling of well-being at its face value instead of as the euphrasy—the false elation—which precedes collapse. Persons far advanced in alcoholism know that feeling. So do tuberculosis patients, and those suffering from severe nervous complaints. It is Nature's way of preparing the afflicted for the ordeal of breakdown.

Being triply prepared, for reasons you may probably guess, I felt triply good.

On Friday afternoon of the next-to-the-last week of school, I paused at the doorway of a study hall, called gayly to the girl inside, then—moved by a sudden hunch—went in and joined her.

"How you doing, Gladys?" I said. "Keeping you in after school, are they?"

"N-no." She tittered shyly. "Everyone's so busy getting ready for graduation that they asked me to help with this stuff."

She was a bashful, dowdy girl, one of those helplessly homely drudges who knew everything in the books and little outside of them, and who would go through life in some minor, ill-rewarded capacity. I had known her in several classes, during my periods of self-promotion, and while I was a different type of outcast I sympathized with and felt sorry for her. Because she was shy and obliging, she was constantly being imposed on. The school employees were always dragging her in on jobs which they were paid to do.

"Making out report cards, huh?" I said. "Like to have me read the record cards off to you? You can go a lot faster that way."

"We-el—" She tittered again. "If you're sure you want to."

"There's nothing I want to do more," I said truthfully. And dragging a chair up to the desk, I sat down at her side.

I took charge of the record file, and began calling the names and grades off to her. Coming to my card, I made myself a senior and gave myself passing grades in every subject.

She looked up, a faint frown on her face. "I—uh—I didn't know that—"

"Yes?" I said.

"Nothing. I mean, I was just going to say how funny it is

that people can be in the same grade and have different teachers for every subject."

"Well," I shrugged, "it's a big school. Incidentally, some of these record cards are pretty badly worn. I think we'd better make out some new ones."

I pulled a dozen odd cards from the file, sliding my own in among them. Somewhat troubled, she began making out new cards from the information I gave her.

I called out my name. I called out the class—senior, second semester. I started calling off credit hours.

Slowly, she laid down her pen and looked up again.

"J-James, you can't. You're not going to graduate, are you? The diploma list is already made out, and I d-don't believe I saw your name on—"

"No," I said. "I'm not going to graduate, Gladys."

"B-but—"

"I don't have enough credit hours to graduate," I said. "Just enough for college entrance."

"Y-yes, but—"

"That isn't much, is it? I've gone to school here for six years. I've made some of the highest grades ever made by a senior. But I still can't graduate. All I have is enough credits to go to college—if I ever have the chance to go. Does that seem like a lot to you? Do you think it's too much, Gladys?"

She looked at me steadily. Then, slowly, she shook her head.

"No," she said, "I don't think it's too much." And she picked up the pen again.

A new card went into the file, one of more than a dozen. It gave me fourteen and a half credit hours, one and a half short of the number necessary to graduate.

I took all the old cards with me, tearing them up on the way home.

Thus, I finished high school. Just before, figuratively speaking, I was finished.

I hadn't been home an hour when the good feeling rushed from me like water rushing down a drain. Then, after a long moment of absolute emptiness, my heart stuttered and raced, beating faster and faster until one beat overlapped the other. Blood gushed from my mouth and I fell to the floor in convulsions.

Doctors came, although I was unaware of their presence. They administered to me wonderingly. I was eighteen years old, and I had a complete nervous collapse, pulmonary tuberculosis and delirium tremens.

# XXIII

FROM A PURELY medical standpoint, I should have died. In fact, I should have been dead long before. I seemed to be completely drained of physical resistance. Well over six feet tall, I weighed less than a hundred and ten pounds. And a good part of that weight, in the doctors' estimation, appeared to be scar tissue. My kidneys were bruised. My ribs floated. My skull had been fractured in three places. I had an incipient rupture. My shoulders were sprained so that the arms did not articulate properly in their sockets. My knuckles had been "knocked down," my fingers broken. Nothing about me was as it should be, physically speaking. As the doctors saw it, I had nothing with which to battle the diseases from which I was suffering.

Fortunately for me, I come from very rugged stock. On both sides of the family, my ancestors were a tough stubborn people. Migrating from England to Ireland to Holland and thence to America, they drifted westward from Pennsylvania—after the revolution against King George—and the farther west they went, the tougher and more stubborn they seemed to get. They regarded illness and injury as annoyances, and succumbing to them, weakness. Many had died violent deaths, few of any infirmity but old age.

So, while I was bedfast for several months, I lived. Because the will-to-live was bred into me. Because I was too stubborn to die.

My illness, and the financial crisis it precipitated, was not without its bright side. It forced us to do things which we should have done long before. We gave up our home and its furnishings, and moved into a rented house in a working-class neighborhood. Thus, we were simultaneously freed of oppressive interest payments and the necessity of maintaining "face" among people who had known us when.

We could live on half the amount we had formerly spent. We were free forever from our most avaricious and persistent creditors. Pop worried less and was able to move about more freely. He made several fast lease deals which, though small, were enough to keep us going.

After a convalescence of some four months, I was able to be up and about, taking care of myself instead of being taken care of. But I was still very weak and thin, and the doctors were not at all pleased with the state of my lungs. I would never recover, in their opinion, in the low, damp climate of Fort Worth. I belonged in a high and dry altitude, and the quicker I got to it the better.

So, early one morning, I stood at the edge of the highway on the outskirts of Fort Worth, one arm supporting an upstretched thumb, the other clutching a small bundle. There was a change of clothing in it, toothbrush and razor, a nickel table and pencils. That was about all.

A car stopped. The driver swung the door open, and I climbed in.

"Where you going, kid?"

"West," I said.

"How far?"

"A long ways. I don't know exactly."

"Lookin' for work? What kinda line you in?"

"I'm a writer," I said. And somehow my voice rose. "I'm a writer!"

"Sure, now," he said, amiably. "Sure you are."

We sped down the highway, and the sun rose behind us, warm, friendly, gentle, silvering the long asphalt ribbon to the west.

I spent more than three years in West and Far West Texas. A bum and casual laborer at first, an itinerant but solvent worker later. In the beginning, I thought it one of the most desolate areas in the world, populated by the world's most arrogant and high-handed people. Only harsh necessity kept me there. As time went on, however, I came to love the vast stretches of prairie, rolling emptily toward the horizon. There was peace in the loneliness, calm and reassurance. In this virgin vastness, virtually unchanged by the assaults of a hundred million years, troubles seemed to shrink and hope loomed large. Everything would go on, one knew, and man would go on with it. Disappointment and difficulty were only way stops on the road to a happy destination.

As for the West Texans, I became every bit as fond of them as I was of the land they lived in. They were not quite so much arrogant, I found, as plain-spoken. Their first say-so on a subject was also their last one. They said what they meant—whether painful or pleasant—and they meant what they said. No snub was implied by silence. It meant only that the West Texan concerned had nothing to say.

One day, a few weeks after leaving Fort Worth, I went into a store in the then village of Big Springs to buy a work shirt. The proprietor tossed one on the counter. The price, he said, was two dollars and fifty cents.

"What!" I exclaimed. "Two-fifty for just a plain blue work shirt?"

"You want it?" he asked.

"Well, no. I can't pay—"

"Reckon we're kind of wastin' time, then," he said, casually, and he tossed the shirt back on the shelf.

Red-faced, my ears burning, I turned and walked away.

I had reached the door when he called to me, still in that casually indifferent tone. I hesitated, then I turned around and went back.

"What price shirt was you lookin' for, bub?" he said. "Somethin' about a dollar?"

"About that," I nodded. "But—"

"Think I got one left. Yeah, here it is."

He took it off the shelf—the two-fifty shirt—and began wrapping it up. "How about some pants?" he said. "That pair you got on is just about the most ragged-assed I ever seen."

I laughed unwillingly. "I guess not. They're pretty bad all right, but—"

"Call it a dollar for the shirt *and* pants," he said. "What size you wear, bub?"

He wrapped the two garments, tossed them to me and raised his hand in an indifferent salute. I thanked him, telling him I would be in to pay what I owed as soon as I could.

"Glad to see you, bub," he nodded. "Don't owe me nothin', though."

"But the shirt alone was—"

"It and the pants was one buck. I set my own prices, bub. Don't need no one to help me."

"Well, I—I see," I said.

"So long," he said, and without another word he slouched back to the rear of the store.

Thus, your typical West Texan—a man who might give you a mile but who would not give in to you an inch. They seldom smiled, those West Texans, and I don't recall ever hearing one laugh. Yet they had a wonderful sense of humor. Their wit was of a dry, back-handed sort, based in antiexaggeration and understatement—delightful once you understood it, baffling and even a little terrifying to an outsider.

One of my earlier positions was as a "sweater" in an oil field gambling house. A sweater, as you may know, is one grade above a bum—a person tolerated by the management for making himself useful to the customers. He is allowed to sleep on the dice tables at night. Now and then, when he hustles a round of drinks or sandwiches, the players toss him a chip. The job is obviously a precarious one, and the man who holds it is usually the possessor of a large thirst. Hence, he is in a more or less constant state of anxiety. Figuratively, and often literally, he sweats.

This place was about twenty miles out of the county seat of Big Springs, and late one night it was raided by a party of deputy sheriffs. Players and house employees resisted furiously. The lights were shot out, and bullets, bludgeons and bottles crashed and thudded in the darkness. Unable to see who was whom, everyone began an indiscriminate slugging of everyone else.

I crawled behind the bar and eventually made my way out to the roof and down to the ground. Here I was grabbed by an old rancher who was loading his ancient touring car with casualties from the brawl.

"Give me a hand with these fellas, slim boy," he said. "Gotta get 'em in town to a doctor."

I demurred, at first, feeling more than a little shaky. But the rancher had thoughtfully "borried" a quantity of potables from the bar, and being liberally refreshed with these I soon fell to with a will.

We piled the combatants into the car, my companion merrily insisting that there was always room for one more, and roared off toward town.

The road was a former cowpath, now deeply rutted by trucks and filled with sinkholes and washouts. As the car bounced and sailed into the air, landing with bone-breaking violence, groans arose from our cargo.

The rancher frowned with annoyance. He increased his speed, and the groans increased. They became yells, shrieks, curses. Some of the awfullest profanity I have ever heard filled the night.

Grimly, my friend emptied the bottle he had been drinking from and handed it to me. "Bunch o' dirty mouths," he scowled. "Give 'em what for, slim boy. Make 'em quiet down."

"Oh, I don't think I'd better," I said. "After all, they're hurt."

"Fellas that yells that loud ain't hurt much. Give 'em somethin' to fuss about!"

"But they're cops, deputy sheriffs. They'll—"

"*Huh!*" He slammed on the brakes. "I thought they was sportin' fellas!"

Grumbling angrily, he took a shotgun from the floor boards of the car and climbed out. Sternly, he ordered the thoroughly revived deputies to unload.

They did so. He lined them up in front of the headlights of the car, examined them briefly and declared them physically fit.

"Danged ornery coyotes," he said, bitterly. "Buttin' in on a nice friendly game! Takin' advantage of a pore ol' man what can't see good! I'll learn you, by gadfrey. You want to get to town, start walkin'!"

It was ten miles into town, a greater distance perhaps than many of the saddle-born, boot-shod deputies had walked in their entire lives. Moreover, as one of them pointed out, it was almost impossible to see where one was walking.

"Hadn't ought to do this to us, Jeb," he protested. "A dark night like this a fella's liable to step spang onto a rattle-snake."

"Don't give a dang if you do," the rancher retorted. "Never liked rattlesnakes nohow!"

We left them there on the prairie, and drove back for a load of gamblers. More than three hours later, we passed the deputies as they limped into the outskirts of Big Springs.

Fearing repercussions, I was not very conspicuous around the gambling hall for the ensuing week. But my trepidation seemed unwarranted. The deputies dropped in for drinks and a hand of cards, amiably admitting their error in raiding the place. "Just plumb bit off more'n we could chew," they said. "Didn't have no idee they'd be so many o' you fellas around." Their attitude was, generally, that they had perpe-trated a joke which had backfired on them.

And exactly two weeks from the date of the first raid, they raided the place again.

One man was killed in attempting to escape. Two others were critically wounded. Then, with the remaining habitués under arrest, the deputies took axes and chopped the gam-bling hall into kindling. All this quite casually—as politely as circumstances would permit. They had taken the joke that was played on them. Now, they were returning it.

Fortunately, I had stopped "sweating" the night before and was not among those present.

# XXIV

M Y NEW JOB was with a salvage contractor, a man who bought abandoned derricks and dismantled them for their lumber. It was quite a profitable business, lumber being a high-priced commodity in the plains areas, and he paid his employees well. But none of them worked for him very long. Those who did not have the good sense to quit when they saw what was required of them inevitably fell victim to the laws of gravity.

I was put next to the job by a character named Strawlegs, a one-time banjo player and an all-time dipsomaniac. He brushed over the nature of the work lightly, emphasizing only the money to be made. But even had I known nothing of the oil fields—and I knew quite a bit—I would have known that the job was dangerous.

"You're dead wrong," Strawlegs insisted, "and I'll prove it to you. Grab ahold of that porch roof, there. That's right, pull your feet up. Now, you're all right, aren't you? You can do it, can't you?"

"But I'm only a few inches off the ground."

"What's the difference, as long as you don't let go? It wouldn't be any harder if you were a few feet up."

"Or a hundred and ten," I suggested sardonically.

Well, I took the job, needing money badly. And Strawlegs, who was then the contractor's only other employee, received fifty dollars for recruiting me.

My survival, during the subsequent several weeks, can only be credited to a miracle.

We would climb to the top of a derrick, lugging tools and ropes with us. Then, perched more than a hundred feet in the air, we would weave ropes through the crown block, and swing off into space. The ropes could not be tied around us, of course. They were wrapped around our waists in a half-hitch which we snubbed with our feet.

We would swing down to the first crosspieces, get a lowering rope around them, and knock and pry them loose at one end. Then, we would swing over to the other end, hang on with one hand and knock and pry with the other, eventually lowering the lumber to the ground.

There are four sides to a derrick, of course. Strawlegs and I each took two, always careful to work opposite each other. In this way, neither side became weaker than the others, and the great tower did not immediately react to the loss of its bracing. It was not until you were about a third of the way down, a mere eighty feet or so above the sagebrush and cactus, that weird and frightening things began to happen.

The giant legs of the derrick would start shivering, first one, then another, until they were all shivering in unison. Then, with ominous gentleness, one side would lean forward and the other backward, swinging you in through the tower or swaying you out of it. And just when you were sure that it was going to topple, carrying you with it, it would straighten again and lean over another way. When it wasn't shivering it was leaning, and when it wasn't leaning it was dancing, shimmying in a crazy cater-cornered way. Finally, as you neared the bottom, it was doing all three. There was virtually nothing to hold the huge beams in place, and they showed their freedom with such a wild swaying and pitching that it was all one could do to hold on.

Usually, we did not take out the last crosspieces. As the contractor put it, there was no use in taking chances.

We slid down past them, scurried out of the tower and cut the guy wires on one side. Then we ran, and the tall timber skeleton collapsed with an earth-shaking crash.

Because the work was always a long ways from town, Strawlegs and I usually lived on the job, setting up batch in the inevitable tool shed. Now and then, however, we had to or felt we had to go into Big Springs. And on one such occasion we got involved in a donnybrook. I can't say how it started, and I doubt that any of the other participants could. It was just one of those things that happen when too many men get too much to drink. Anyway, Strawlegs got a fractured skull out of it and had to be taken to a hospital, and I got knocked through a plate-glass window.

A party of deputies began collaring the miscreants. One of them laid hands on me and hustled me toward his car.

"But I haven't done anything!" I said, not too truthfully. "You think I like getting knocked through windows?"

"Shoulda aimed yourself better," he said. "Ought to been ziggin' when you was zaggin'."

"That's not very damned funny," I said. "I get—"

"And that's a fact," he nodded soberly. "You wanta move or you want me to move you?"

I was fined eighteen dollars for disturbing the peace. Then, much to my amazement, I was given three days to pay up and released without bond.

I passed the deputy on the way out of the courthouse. "See you soon," he said.

"Sure, you'll see me all right," I said.

"I'll see you," he said. "And that's a fact."

The derrick we were working on was forty miles from town. It had been erected more than ten years before, and the trail to it was so overgrown and eroded that it was practically impossible to see, let alone traverse. Even the contractor had lost his way several times, and wound up in another county. It was spring-breaking, low-gear going for a stout truck.

I was sure that the deputy would never find that trail, nor get to the end of it if he did find it.

The morning of the fourth day arrived. The contractor was off scouting another job. Strawlegs was still in the hospital. I was up in the derrick, rigging the ropes and removing shivs from the crown block, when a car came over the horizon. It was listing to one side, steam pluming from the radiator, and it clattered deafeningly.

It stopped fifty yards or so away, and the deputy got out. He waved to me, then sauntered up to the derrick floor, teetering in his high-heeled boots.

"Howdy," he called upward, and waited. "Dropped around to see your buddy yesterday. Said to tell you he was feeling fine."

I stared down at him. Finally, I found my voice. "Have a nice ride?"

"Tol'able. Left town last night."

"Well, here I am," I said. "Come on and get me."

"Ain't in no hurry. Just as soon rest a spell."

"Why don't you shoot me?" I said. "I'm a pretty desperate criminal."

"Ain't got no gun." He grinned up at me lazily. "Never seen much sense in shooting. And that's a fact."

He stretched out on the derrick floor and put his hands under his head. He closed his eyes.

I sat on a crosspiece for a while, smoking. Then I climbed up to the top of the rig and took the hatchet from my belt. I chopped at the edge of the crown block, sending down a shower of grease-soaked splinters.

He brushed them off, lazily, pulling his hat over his face.

I chopped out a small piece of the block, catching it in my hand before it could fall. I took careful aim and let go.

It struck near the side of his head, bounced into the air and landed between his folded hands. He sat up. He looked up at me, then looked at the piece of wood. He took out his pocketknife and began to whittle.

There is always a wind in West Texas. It blows relentlessly, straight off the North Pole in winter, straight out of hell in summer. It was summer now, early summer. The wind rolled through the derrick at a baking, dehydrating one hundred and twenty degrees. There was no protection from it. I had no water. By noon I was getting dizzy, and my throat felt like it had been blistered.

The deputy stood up, looked around and sauntered into the tool shed. Some fifteen minutes later he came out, wiping his mouth with the back of his hand.

"Like to have some chow?" he called. "A little water?"

"You kidding?" I croaked.

"I'll find a pail. You can pull it up on the rope."

He started for the tool shed again. In spite of myself, I laughed.

"Let it go," I said. "I'm coming down."

He was a good-looking guy. His hair was coal-black beneath his pushed-back Stetson, and his black intelligent eyes were set wide apart in a tanned, fine-featured face. He grinned at me as I dropped down in front of him on the derrick floor.

"Now, that wasn't very smart," he said. "And that's—"

"And that's a fact," I snapped. "All right, let's get going."

He went on grinning at me. In fact, his grin broadened a little. But it was fixed, humorless, and a veil seemed to drop over his eyes.

"What makes you so sure," he said, softly, "you're going anywhere?"

"Well, I—" I gulped. "I—I—"

"Awful lonesome out here, ain't it? Ain't another soul for miles around but you and me."

"L-look," I said. "I'm—I wasn't trying to—"

"Lived here all my life," he went on, softly. "Everyone knows me. No one knows you. And we're all alone. What do you make o' that, a smart fella like you? You've been around. You're all full of piss and high spirits. What do you think an ol' stupid country boy might do in a case like this?"

He stared at me, steadily, the grin baring his teeth. I stood paralyzed and wordless, a great cold lump forming in my stomach. The wind whined and moaned through the derrick. He spoke again, as though in answer to a point I had raised.

"Don't need one," he said. "Ain't nothin' you can do with a gun that you can't do a better way. Don't see nothin' around here I'd need a gun for."

He shifted his feet slightly. The muscles in his shoulders bunched. He took a pair of black kid gloves from his pocket, and drew them on, slowly. He smacked his fist into the palm of his other hand.

"I'll tell you something," he said. "Tell you a couple of things. There ain't no way of telling what a man is by looking at him. There ain't no way of knowing what he'll do if he has the chance. You think maybe you can remember that?"

I couldn't speak, but I managed a nod. His grin and his eyes went back to normal.

"Look kind of peaked," he said. "Why'n't you have somethin' to eat an' drink before we leave?"

I paid my fine. I also paid for a bench warrant, the deputy's per diem for two days and his mileage. And you can be sure that I made no fuss about it.

I never saw that deputy again, but I couldn't get him out of my mind. And the longer he remained there the bigger riddle he presented. Had he been bluffing? Had he only meant to throw a good scare into a brash kid? Or was it the other way, the way I was sure it was at the time? Had my meekness saved me from the murder with which he had threatened me?

Suppose I had hit him with that block of wood? Suppose I had razzed him a little more? Suppose I had been frightened into grabbing for my hatchet?

I tried to get him down on paper, to put him into a story, but while he was very real to me I could not make him seem real. Rather, he was too commonplace and innocuous—nothing more than another small-town deputy. Put down on paper, he was only solemnly irritated, not murderous.

The riddle, of course, lay not so much in him as me. I tended to see things in black and white, with no intermediate shadings. I was too prone to categorize—naturally, using myself as the norm. The deputy had behaved first one way, then another, then the first again. And in my ignorance I saw this as complexity instead of simplicity.

He had gone as far as his background and breeding would allow to be amiable. I hadn't responded to it, so he had taken another tack. It was simple once I saw things through his eyes instead of my own.

I didn't know whether he would have killed me, because he didn't know himself.

Finally, as I matured, I was able to re-create him on paper

—the sardonic, likeable murderer of my fourth novel, *The Killer Inside Me*. But I was a long time in doing it—almost thirty years.

And I still haven't got him out of my mind.

# XXV

WHILE THE DERRICK dismantling was dangerous, it was not particularly arduous as oil field jobs went. The contractor didn't hurry us. There was a chance to rest between jobs. We worked a few days, and laid off a few—a situation perfectly suited to a man who was not in the best of health. So, though I swore to quit daily, I stayed on for weeks.

Strawlegs and I were fairly well-heeled when winter came on, and we were forced to quit. Because jobs generally had to be scrounged for in the oil fields and transportation service was nonexistent, we bought an old Model-T touring car.

We odd-jobbed through the boom towns of Chalk and Foursands, then settled down temporarily on a pipeline job between Midland and Big Springs. The pay was fair—four-fifty a day less a dollar deducted for "slop and flop."

The bosses were hard men, but they were not slave drivers. Still, I soon had more of the job than I could take, and so had Strawlegs. Neither of us was physically capable of swinging a shovel and pick for nine hours a day, seven days a week.

Winter was with us, however. We had very little money and no other prospects for work. The only thing to do, seemingly, was to stay here without working. So, after many inquiries and a careful study of camp routine, we did that.

The bosses assumed, naturally, that everyone in camp was working. It followed then that everyone would have earnings from which the dollar-a-day could be deducted, and no head-count was made at meal times. Thus, to eat and sleep free, it was only necessary to keep out of sight during working hours. Immediately after breakfast, Strawlegs and I slipped off into the underbrush, remaining there until lunch time. After lunch we disappeared again, and returned for supper and the night.

Strawlegs was well-educated and had traveled widely and well before booze got the best of him. We both shared a deep interest in the nominally inconsequential, and could spend hours discussing the stamen of a sage bloom or the antics of an ant.

There were four hundred men in the camp—drifters, bums, jailbirds, fugitives from justice. Of necessity, such camps were always isolated and they moved in and out of counties as the work progressed. It was impossible for the local authorities to police them, so the camp bosses did the job. Sometimes they were deputized, sometimes not. In any case they dispensed a pretty fair brand of justice.

Gamblers and bootleggers followed the job, traveling in cars and setting up their own tents on the outskirts of camp. They were allowed to operate freely, as long as they did it at night and behaved themselves. The bootlegger's product had to be good, and his prices reasonable. The consistently "lucky" gambler was quickly spotted and eliminated.

More than once I have seen a boss ("man with the stroke") step up to a crap or blackjack table and order the proprietor to pack and get. There would be no explanation beyond, possibly, "You've got enough," or "knock off while you're able to." And I never knew of but one gambler to object. The words were hardly out of his mouth before a fist landed on it and a boot landed under his table, scattering chips, cards and cash to the wind.

One night two whores drifted into camp and were promptly ordered to leave. The bosses were somewhat more explanatory about this edict than others since "ladies" were involved. They pointed out that the men were generally a rough and ready lot who would certainly look upon the women as fair and free game. The two would get nothing for their trouble but exercise, and much more of that than they wanted.

Well, the women left, but sullenly. And late that night they slipped back into camp. The forty men in the first of the ten tents took charge of them. They got no farther, and they almost didn't get out of it alive.

As their wild shrieks ripped through the night, the "strokes" leaped cursing from their cots. They jerked on their boots, snatched up pick handles and advanced on Number One tent on the run. But there were only ten of them, and many of the men in adjoining tents sided with the occupants of the first one. The onslaught of the bosses was met with clubs, knives, cot legs and razors. As fast as one workman went down, his head split open by a whizzing pick handle, two more sprang forward to take his place.

But the pipeliners didn't have to win, and the strokes did have to. Otherwise, they were through in the oil fields. So, finally, they formed a ring around the mauled and hysterical women and fought their way out of camp.

The camp set an abundant table in the hundred-yard-long dining tent. There were usually three kinds of meat, even at breakfast. In addition to meat, the average lunch and dinner included a half-dozen vegetables, cornbread, biscuits and light bread, coffee and milk, pie, cake and fruit. But preparing twelve hundred huge meals a day under primitive conditions was something to test a saint, and pipeline cooks were very far from sainthood. Thus, despite good raw materials, the end product was not always good. And despite the variety and abundance, one did not always get what he wanted or as much as he wanted.

It was hard to get a dish passed. When it was passed, it was likely to be emptied before it got to the man who requested it. So the moment they sat down at the table, the men started grabbing meat, potatoes and cake—whatever was nearest them. And fearful that they might get nothing more, they dumped the contents of the bowl or platter onto their own plates. One man would have eight or nine pounds of meat in front of him, another a gallon of potatoes, another a whole cake and so on.

The flunkies (waiters) rushed more food to the table, refills of the original dishes. But these likewise were apt to proceed no farther than the men who grabbed them. They would simply throw away the remainder of the uneaten cake, meat or potatoes and empty the second dish onto their plates. Inevitably, much more food went under the table than into the men's stomachs.

The bosses did what they could to correct the situation, but they were never completely successful. The cooks—invariably hard-drinking, short-tempered men—grew murderous. They botched food, deliberately. They threw dirt into it. Sometimes they did worse.

One night we were served great platters of golden brown, "breaded" pork chops. There were so many of them that even the greediest men could see that there was plenty for all, and every man was able to fill his plate. Then, they cut into the chops, and the meat almost dripped with blood. It hadn't been cooked, only browned lightly on the side.

Outraged and profane yells rose from the table. Snatching up handfuls of the bloody pork, the men rushed toward the rear of the tent where the meals were prepared. The cooks stopped their charge temporarily with hurled kettles of boiling food. Then, before their would-be murderers could fully recover, the culinary staff fled the tent as one man, scampering across the prairie in their white uniforms and caps like so many overstuffed, outsize jack-rabbits.

I imagine that they were later picked up and driven into town by some of the bosses. At any rate, they did not return to camp, and a new batch of cooks was brought in in time to cook the morning meal.

# XXVI

B Y WORKING AS a team at the table, Strawlegs and I
fared uncommonly well, and the abundance of food
combined with the long days of rest did wonders for
us. We moved on, when the job ended in mid-winter, very
nearly broke but in better health than we had enjoyed for a
long time.

We went back to Foursands. There was no work there so,
after a few days, we went to the town of Midland.

We found no work here either, not enough to support us.
Finally, much against our better judgment, we sold a third
interest in the car to a man named Bragg.

I learned two very valuable things from this transaction.
First, that when things get so bad they are about to get better; second, that no bargain is better than a bad one. The day
after the deal was made we got work on a highline job, but
Bragg would not allow us to buy him out. We were stuck

with him, and if there was ever an undesirable partner to have in anything he was it.

He was a giant of a man, more than six feet six inches tall, more than two hundred and fifty pounds of almost solid muscle. And every ounce and inch of him was packed with unadulterated meanness.

Bragg publicly addressed us as "turds" and "turdheads." He would talk about revolting subjects at mealtimes, making us sick to our stomachs. He was forever knocking us breathless with slaps on the back or bumping into us in such a way as to send us sprawling. Then, he would insist on shaking hands—crushing our fingers until we were forced to grovel.

I remarked a few pages back that no one is wholly bad, but if Bragg had a single redeeming feature I don't know what it was. The nicest thing I can say about him is that he was a no-good, double-dyed, rotten son-of-a-bitch.

We had to live on the job, sleeping and cooking out when the weather permitted, shacking-up in the nearest tool house when it did not. Bragg bedded down on the cushions of the car, and covered himself with the side curtains. Strawlegs and I had to make do with our blankets. Bragg ate two-thirds of the food or more. He paid for a third or less—and sometimes he would pay for nothing.

It was always our fault whenever anything went wrong with the car. Bragg would neither pay for repairs nor let them go unmade.

About the only work Strawlegs and I could do was with the pick and shovel, digging the holes for the highline towers. Bragg, however, was skilled at several kinds of the work involved. He worked steadily—two days to our one. While we were often too hard up to buy cigarettes, he saved money hand over fist.

He would take the car with him on days when we were not working, returning at nightfall like as not with a broken spring or a blown-out tire which, of course, he blamed on us. Bragg's idea of a hilarious joke was to leave us out on the prairie all day, dozens of miles from town, without food or water.

Knowing of nothing else to do, Strawlegs and I stayed on—hopefully, at first, thinking that things might improve, then, out of pure stubbornness. Obviously, Bragg wanted us to give up and move on, leaving him in possession of the car. So, though it was a losing proposition for us, we stayed.

When the highline job ended in the spring, we suggested selling the car and dividing the proceeds. Bragg flatly refused. He was going on to the town of Rankin, he said, to an impending pipeline job. We could do as we pleased, but he was going in the car, necessarily taking our two-thirds with his third.

Strawlegs and I decided to go to Rankin.

It lay seventy miles to the west, and there was not a filling station nor house throughout the distance. The road was a rutted, red clay trail, stretching through a dry, sparsely grassed desert.

We had two blowouts in the first ten miles. By nightfall we were only halfway to our destination. We had to stop then, since we could not proceed fast enough for the magneto-powered lights to function. Pitching camp at the side of the trail, Strawlegs and I were allowed a little bread and bologna and water. Bragg took charge of the rest.

When morning came, he finished what remained of the food and water, and ensconced himself comfortably in the back seat. With his feet in our necks and nothing in our stomach, we continued on our way.

We didn't continue far before the radiator began to boil, and cursing us for the lack of water, Bragg ordered a stop. We let the engine cool a while, and drove on again. A few more miles and the overheated motor again forced us to stop.

Bragg got out of the car and hauled us out. Perching himself precariously on the front spring, he unscrewed the cap of the radiator and urinated in it. He stepped down, grimly, advising us to emulate his example.

We did, insofar as we were able to. But we had had very little water and the drying wind had taken most of that from us. For all Bragg's cursings and poundings on the back, we could not produce something we did not have.

We drove another ten miles, perhaps, before the red-hot engine again forced a halt. And this time there was another difficulty which called for water. Our joltings and the climate had loosened the spokes of the right rear wheel. Unless they were soaked and allowed to swell, the wheel would soon fall apart.

Bragg cursed us until his throat was hoarse. He grabbed us by the neck and bumped our heads together.

"Smart bastards," he grunted. "Just look what you went and done! Whatcha going to do now?"

"You can have my share in the wreck," I said, for it would cost far more to repair now than it was worth. "I'm going to walk on into town."

"That goes for me, too," said Strawlegs.

"Oh, no you don't," snapped Bragg. "You ain't givin' me your share—not now, anyways—and you ain't goin' off to town after water. We're goin' to carry it in, me and you turds, and you're damned well goin' to carry your share."

"*Carry it!*" We stared at him incredulously. "Carry the—*it?*"

"Carry the car. Grab onto it!"

Well, we carried it, the right side of it, that is. With Strawlegs and I at the front wheel, elevating the heavier section, and Bragg at the rear, we lugged the car the ten miles into town.

Strawlegs and I were more dead than alive when we got

there. But, with Bragg prodding and threatening us, we managed to get the old Ford into a junk yard. The proprietor gave us ten dollars for it, distributing the money himself so that Strawlegs and I got our share.

This was not Bragg's idea of a fair way to divide things, but there was not much he could do about it. There were hundreds of pipeliners in town, men we had known from the last job. He could not get tough with us without becoming painfully involved with them. Moreover, I think he saw that he had pushed us just about as far as he could and that he would either have to kill or be killed if he didn't leave us alone.

So, he parted from us, with many curses and threats, and we never saw him again, neither in town or out of it. The pipeline job was not nearly so imminent as it had been rumored to be, and I imagine he decided not to wait for it.

With no work immediately available in Rankin, Strawlegs and I caught a ride to McCamey. An orchestra was winding up its engagement in the town, and Strawlegs had known the leader in better days. The latter offered him a job as a banjo player, and, at my urging, he took it. It meant the parting of the ways for us, of course, but that parting was not too far off at best. Certainly, I did not intend to tramp through the oil fields any longer than I had to.

Strawlegs was a very good banjo player, as, if you have guessed his right name, you know. He was also a very good little guy. On the last night of the orchestra's engagement in McCamey, he met me outside the dance hall and pressed his earnings to date upon me.

"You'll need this before you find work," he insisted. "Anyway, you've got it coming to you."

He then revealed that he had gotten fifty dollars from the derrick-salvaging contractor for recruiting me. So, seeing him conscience-stricken over the deed and greatly concerned for my welfare, I took the money and we said goodbye.

The hiring office for the projected pipeline was at Rankin, but construction of the line was to begin near the town of Iran, extending from there to the Gulf of Mexico. I went there, finding no work in McCamey and a hundred men for every job in Rankin.

Iran was far Far West Texas—a handful of false front buildings and a few dozen people dropped down in the middle of nowhere. The town had once been the center of a shallow oil field, but now there was almost no drilling activity. It existed largely as a stop on the stage lines west and as a trading post for ranchers.

Obviously, the residents had little for themselves, but what little they had they shared. They were a more sharply drawn version, an emphasized extension of their brethren West Texans. I was so touched by their kindness and reluctant to impose upon it that I stayed outside of town as much as possible.

With a few cans of food, coffee, flour and salt pork, I "jungled up" on a table rock overlooking the Pecos River, cooking in a lard can, sleeping with my back to a low fire. I was safe there from the rattlesnakes and other poisonous creatures which infested the area. Now and then at night I had brief spells of delirium tremens—a recurrent form which sometimes afflicts a person long after he has stopped drinking—but they were never severe. Almost as soon as I started yelling, the illusion of things crawling over me vanished.

I wrote a great deal during the days—vignettes, sketches of people I had met. Most of what I wrote I tore up. I passed the days writing, thinking, swimming in the river, eating and sleeping. So the long summer waned, and fall came.

Construction on the pipeline began. I was given the job of guarding it at night.

I don't know why. There was nothing about me that would have intimidated the most timid malefactor, and I had never fired a gun in my life.

# XXVII

A FEW YEARS ago, before I began to fight back at booze instead of merely fighting it, I was a patient in a West Coast sanitarium for alcoholics. I had become a habitué of such places, as had many of my fellow patients. By way of whiling away the time, we took turns at relating the horrific adventures which alcohol had gotten us into.

One man—an actor—had inadvertently crawled into the Pullman berth occupied by a heavyweight fighter and his wife.

A reporter had bedded down in a garbage wagon and was dumped into a penful of hungry hogs.

A writer, gripped by a fit of vomiting, had become lodged head and shoulders in a toilet seat and had to be extricated with crowbars.

One of the best, or, at least, the funniest stories was told by a Hollywood director, a sad-eyed little man who was given to spells of extreme melancholia.

For years, when he reached a certain stage of saturation, he would telephone the newspapers and announce that he was about to commit suicide. He really meant to when he made the calls, but by the time the reporters arrived he was always out of the notion.

The reporters and photographers became very irritated with him. The least he could do, they declared, was to scratch himself up a little or take a few too many sleeping pills, or do something they could make a story out of.

But the director adamantly resisted their pleadings and cursings and jeerings. Scratch himself? Horrors! He might get an infection. Sleeping pills? Never! They gave him a stomach-ache.

Now, the local reporters always had more than their fill of Hollywood characters, and this guy seemed to be a little too much to bear. They couldn't ignore him. He was an important man, and there was always the chance that he might decide to go through—or partly through—with his threat.

Every newspaper man in town was burned up with him. Along toward the last, the desk men were conversing with him somewhat as follows:

"Now, Bob, you've disappointed us very badly. I'm afraid we can't believe you any more unless you give us at least a little evidence of good faith."

"I will!" the director would sob. "Honestly, I will. I know I haven't done the right thing by you boys, but I'm going to make up for it now."

"Well"—the editor would hesitate fretfully—"I'll give you one more chance to make good."

The director summoned them late one night, deciding as usual, after they arrived, that neither death nor its approaches seemed attractive. But before the first trembling syllables passed his lips, the reporters grabbed him.

Cackling with insane glee, they begged him not to hang himself. "Don't do it, old friend! Please don't hang yourself!" they shouted. And they removed the cord from his robe and knotted it about his neck.

The reporters stood him up on the end of the bed and tied the cord to the chandelier.

They jerked the bed from beneath him.

The chandelier came loose from its moorings. The director landed on the floor and it landed on top of him. Stunned as he was, he retained enough sense to scramble under the bed and stay there.

"Of course, they didn't intend to actually hang me," he explained, relating the story. "But they did want me strung up long enough to get a picture. And I'll bet those heartless, cold-blooded bastards would have torn down every chandelier in the house to get one!"

The newspaper men spent some time in trying to drag him from beneath the bed. But seeing that he remained obdurate and elusive, and in view of the fact that they had accomplished their purpose of teaching him a lesson, they finally left.

The director emerged into the open.

He wasn't really hurt, but in his dazed and drunken condition he saw himself at death's door. He telephoned for an ambulance. The vehicle arrived and he was loaded in. It sped away again, eventually coming to a long hill. About halfway up the incline, the back doors flew open and the director flew out.

He shot down the hill on the wheeled stretcher. ("I was strapped to the goddamned thing.") By the time he neared the bottom, he was traveling at a really awesome speed. The stretcher swerved suddenly and leaped the ditch. It crashed through a barbed wire fence, ploughed through a fruit orchard and came to rest finally more than a hundred yards from the highway.

The director got the straps unloosened and staggered back to the road. His pajamas in tatters, and much of his epidermis as well, he limped back to his house.

"I looked like a walking pile of hamburger," he said. "There wasn't a spot on me that wasn't black and blue or bleeding. Naturally, I called the newspapers to give them the story of my terrifying experience. They told me to drop dead. I called the hospital. I was going to have them verify the story to the newspapers. They told me to drop dead, too. You see, these bastardly ambulance attendants had lied about me. It scared hell out of them when they saw I was missing, so they picked the stretcher up out of that field and told the hospital authorities that I had refused to leave the house.

"It didn't mean a thing that I was virtually cut to ribbons. Drunks are always messing themselves up. So there I was with the biggest story that ever came out of Hollywood, and I couldn't get a damned line in the newspapers. That was the last time I committed suicide. There just wasn't any point to it. Those suspicious bastards wouldn't give me a write-up if I *did* kill myself!"

I had no adventures which would top that one, but I recounted a couple, anyway. One occurred on the pipeline, as an outgrowth of my recurrent d.t.'s. The other...

...I had gone north to enroll at the University of Nebraska. I had had to leave Texas very hastily—for reasons I will reveal later—and I needed work immediately. I tried the two newspapers in Lincoln (the site of the university). I tried the university press and the branches of two syndicates. Finally, I tried a farm paper. And here the two young assistant editors, instead of delivering the fast brush-off I had gotten elsewhere, looked upon me as though I were something good to eat. They gave me the best chair in the office. They pressed cigarettes upon me. They beamed and cooed over me, nodding significantly to one another.

I should say that I was very well dressed. The hotel had expected its employees to dress well, and I had never regarded good clothes as a luxury. I had on a hundred and fifty dollar suit and thirty-five dollar shoes. An imported topcoat was slung over my arm, and I had pigskin gloves in one hand and a forty-dollar Borsalino hat in the other.

So the editors looked at me and each other, and they thought it "highly possible" that they could give me a job. Not right at the moment, but—

"You're enrolling in the College of Agriculture, of course?"

"Good God, no," I laughed. "I'm going to go into liberal arts. Why would a guy who wants to be a writer go to—?"

The editors started talking to me. No one, but positively no one, enrolled in liberal arts any more. A. B.A. degree had as little academic standing as a diploma from a barber college. The thing to shoot for was a B.Sc. in agriculture. There was a terrific demand for writers who knew agriculture. The government was snatching them up as fast as they graduated. There were splendid openings on farm periodicals. Why, take their own case, for example. They were ag college seniors, and already they had these excellent jobs.

They insisted that I go out to "the house" for dinner to discuss the matter.

Well, I knew nothing of such things. I supposed that a bunch of them were keeping batch at this "house" they spoke of. It dawned on me, as we went up the walk of the splendid edifice, that I had made a mistake. But I didn't know how to get out of it. I still didn't know, hours later, after I had been wined and dined and talked to so much by so many that my head was swimming.

It was the traditional fraternity "rush" and it rushed me right off my feet. They pledged me to the house. They enrolled me in the College of Agriculture. And that was the beginning of one of the most God-awful periods in my harried and exasperating career.

The students were assumed to have a sound general knowledge of farming which I didn't have. I had been too young during my several years on farms to learn anything. Furthermore, my hatred of cows was so great that I detested practically everything connected with farming.

My "brothers" could get me no jobs, naturally. I had to get my own, and plenty of them, to keep up my fraternity assessments. The brothers had all they could do, and then some, to keep me from flunking out.

They didn't mind losing my company, understand, they could have done very well without that. But the house treasury couldn't afford to lose the income which I represented. They had to keep me in the fraternity, hence they had to keep me from flunking.

Like most fraternities, the house had exhaustive files of examination papers, extending back for decades. There were also files on the various faculty members, complete dossiers of their likes, dislikes and eccentricities. So, while one group of brothers worked on me, another turned the heat on my instructors. Wherever they went, the poor devils were surrounded by earnest young men pleading my cause so persistently and insistently that it was impossible to say no to them.

There was one man, however, who did say no—loudly, emphatically and repeatedly. He was a little Italian, an exchange professor in pathology, and he had been sore at me ever since I had dropped my fountain pen into a sixty-pound churn of butter. He said that since it was impossible to dissect me (which he really wanted to do), the next best thing was to flunk me.

He was a hard guy, but the brothers had dealt with these tough babies before. And when, as promised, he flunked me on the mid-term final, they gave him the works. The entire membership of the fraternity turned the heat on him.

The house was powerful on the campus, and the result of the "works" was nothing less than astounding. The professor's mildest jokes in class were greeted with wildly appreciative laughter. His most inane remarks were applauded as pearls of wisdom. He was literally carried about the campus by a horde of young men whose admiration for him was equalled only by their praise of Italy.

The professor began to weaken. They gave him the "killer punch." He was made the guest of honor at a house dinner, and every brother stood up, one at a time, and sang his praises for a minimum ten minutes.

At midnight they chauffeured him home, so flushed with pleasure that his face looked like a beet. And when the escorting party returned, I was informed that I was "in." I was to be given a new examination on the morrow, and I would be certain to pass it.

The news obviously called for a celebration, and we had one. I had a terrific hangover the next morning when I presented myself to the professor.

He was all smiles and mysterious grimaces. Wiggling his eyebrows significantly, he whispered that we would go downtown for the examination. "A ver' fine place, I know," he giggled. "A frien', he has so kin'ly let me use it. Here, where there ees so mooch pipples—"

I had never been able to understand him well—one of the many reasons he had disliked me—but I thought I saw his point. It was Saturday, and a great many students were around. If anything unorthodox was to be done, it was best to do it elsewhere.

We went downtown to a building largely occupied by governmental agencies. At the tenth floor, we walked down the dark corridor to a door near the end. There was no sign on it except an abbreviation as incomprehensible in my fuzzy state as it was uninteresting, and an arrow indicating that the entrance proper was elsewhere. The professor unlocked the door and waved me inside.

The shades were drawn and the room was quite dark. Judging by the heavy leather chairs and the rows of glass-shelved bookcases it was some kind of law office. He led me into an adjoining room, equipped only with a table and several chairs, and turned on the light.

"Ver' nice, yes?" He raised his eyebrows at me. "Zis way there is no complaint. You pass examination—ver' steef. You do it, I do not'ing."

"Yeah," I said. "I guess that's right."

"I lock doors so ees no distorbance. Two hours, yes, I come back."

He left by the door of the other room. I unlimbered the pint of whiskey in my pocket and had a hair of the dog. Sitting down at the table, I took out the list of examination questions.

And I almost fell out of my chair.

I didn't know what had happened—whether he had overestimated my abilities or given me the wrong set of questions, or whether he had decided to play a cruel joke on the brothers and me. But I knew I could never pass this examination. I didn't know the answer to a single question.

I took another long drink, trying to think. I took two more drinks. If I could get in touch with the house, put one of the brothers to work on the cram file—

I looked around the room. I glanced into the other one. No telephone and the doors were locked. I paced back and forth fretfully, too worried to give the professor the cursing he deserved.

I raised the shade and the window, and looked out.

The room faced on a court. Cater-cornered to my window, some five feet away, was another. It was glazed and only raised a few inches, so I could not see what it opened into. But it seemed to me it should be a corridor.

I studied it thoughtfully, raising the bottle again. I came to a decision.

I couldn't jump or step across to that window, but it would be an easy fall-over—a trick I had learned in my derrick-salvaging days. If I didn't make it, of course, if I should slip or miss—

But I had done harder fall-overs before and almost as high up, high enough up to be fatal if I had fallen. Height didn't mean anything in itself. A trick could be done as easily at a hundred feet as at ten.

I climbed out on the ledge, crouching. I straightened until I was almost erect. Feet braced, arms outstretched, I let myself fall.

There was a split second when I was holding on with nothing but my heels, staring down into empty space. Then, my hands smacked down on the wooden base of the window and my fingers gripped the inside.

I raised my head and peered in.

It wasn't a corridor but a restroom. I was looking at an angle into one of the stalls. An elderly woman—a char apparently—was seated on the toilet.

She looked at me. I looked at her. She blinked absently and shook her head. She took off her glasses and blew on them.

I eased my hands back out of the window to the brick ledge outside. Suspended in an aching, shaking arc, holding on with my toes and fingertips, I waited.

And waited.

And waited.

I couldn't go back. I couldn't go on. I could, of course,

but the old gal might drop dead. She undoubtedly would scream her head off. And how could anyone explain a deal like this—crawling through the tenth-floor window of a women's john?

I think I have never heard a sweeter sound than the flushing of that toilet. Unless, that is, it was the click of the hall door as it closed behind her. She had gone without coming near the window. Apparently, she distrusted her eyes as much as she seemed to.

I gripped the inside of the window again, and pulled myself up on the ledge. But I couldn't go on with my plan. The woman was probably working in the corridor, or I might run into someone else. Anyway, I just didn't have the heart for it.

I repeated my fall-over, returning to the room I had come from. I sank down at the table and killed the rest of the bottle.

I was seated there, half-dozing, when the professor arrived.

"We are all feenished, eh? We are . . . Mis-ter Tomseen, where is . . . You have wreet-en noth-eeng!"

"Not a damned noth-eeng," I nodded surlily. "What'd you expect?"

"What deed I"—he choked. His eyes began to bulge. "Mister Tom-seen, why do you theenk I—what do you think this ees?" He waved his arms wildly, the gesture encompassing the other room and the abbreviated legend on the door. "What, Mis-ter Tom-seen? You cannot read, no? You have no eyes, yes?"

He glared. I stared. And, slowly, the terrible truth dawned on me. A friend of his . . . A governmental agency . . . And what kind of agency would a friend of his—?

"Oh," I groaned. "Oh, no!"

"Yes, Mis-ter Tom-seen. Oh, yes. A babe in arms, no. A

drooling idiot, no. They could not do it, too smart they would be. But you—*you*—*!*"

Me, I had done it. I had failed a pathology examination in a pathology *library!*

. . . Now, back to the pipeline.

# XXVIII

STRETCHED OUT ALONG the big ditch, and moving farther and farther into the wilderness as the line progressed, were several hundred thousand dollars' worth of equipment and supplies. There were two ditches, twenty electric generators, a dragline, trucks and tractors. There were gasoline and oil dumps, bins of tires, tubes, spark plugs and a hundred other accessories.

It was my job to guard this stuff.

All night long I tramped up and down the ditch, walking the line above the Pecos at one point. I carried a weatherproof gasoline lantern and a repeating rifle. My instructions were literally to "shoot any son-of-a-bitch that shows his face and ask questions afterward."

I rather liked the job in the beginning. The days were still long, and even at midnight there was a friendly semi-twilight over the prairie. By standing on top of a ditching machine, I could see from one end of the job to the other. Very little walking was necessary, and when I did walk it was with comparative safety. I could see and avoid the rattle-snakes, the tarantulas and the great twelve-inch centipedes who considered this area their own private domain.

These things had been bad enough before the coming of the pipeline, but with its advent they seemed to have gotten ten times worse. They weren't any more numerous, of course, but they were considerably more active. The rever-berations of the machinery shook them in their subterranean apartments. Dynamite blasted out great sections of their cities. The ditches scooped them up—there was one nest of a hundred and sixty rattlesnakes—and hurled them out upon the prairie.

Naturally, they didn't like this a damned bit.

The more foolhardy and determined of them gave battle on the spot: this was their home and they did not intend to be dispossessed. The majority, however, preferred to bide their time. They vanished among the sage and rock, waiting until the earth-shaking machinery stilled its clatter and the sun went down. Then, they came swarming back to seek their former dwelling places and to scare hell out of me.

Having no place to hibernate, they became increasingly active and aggravated as the days shortened and cold weather set in. They crept under the canvas jackets of the generators. They hid in the recesses of machinery. They moved endlessly up and down the line, creeping into the joints of pipe, crawling under the curves of the gasoline drums. I was safe from them nowhere, neither on the ground nor up on the machinery.

I had thought I was completely rid of the d.t.'s—the illu-sions of crawling things. Now, they came back and with increased frequency and intensity.

I fought them in the only way I knew how. I would force myself to walk straight toward the spiders and snakes that loomed in the light of my lantern. Sometimes they would melt away under my boots, and sometimes they would not. Instead of vanishing, a diamond-shaped head would lash out venomously, or a ball of centipedes would explode and swarm up my legs. I would drop my lantern and run, brushing hysterically at myself—run and run, shrieking, until I could run no more.

I gave up fighting. Too often an apparent illusion became reality. I tried to get transferred to a day job, but it was no soap. They could get no one to take my place.

Every morning I told myself that I couldn't take another night. But every night I came back. I had waited all summer for the line to start, and it seemed a shame to quit now. Also, I had invested heavily in winter clothes which would be of no use to me on another job.

So I hung on, night after night, and every night was more agonizing and fearful than its predecessor.

A tarantula bite is not fatal, I understand, only painful. But these evil-looking spiders terrified me more than any of their nightmarish colleagues. They grew to the size of soup plates, and they were furred like rabbits. They could leap like rabbits, too, a dozen feet or more. And they invariably would leap at anything that showed up in the darkness—the lantern, my face and hands.

I never saw one of them alone. There was always at least a pair of them, marching side by side, and sometimes there were squadrons. I lived in mortal fear of them.

Late one night, I was walking the line across the Pecos, moving cautiously to preserve my balance on the snow-covered pipe. I had reached a point about mid-stream when, looking ahead, I saw a double file of pie-shaped blots—a squadron of tarantulas marching straight toward me.

I knew it was an illusion, but—but nothing. If a thing exists in a man's mind, it exists. My heart began to pound wildly. I choked up with terror. I turned around and started to head back toward the other bank. There, marching toward me from that direction, was another tarantula squadron.

I let out a wild yell and plunged from the pipe.

I fell thirty feet, smashing through the ice-sheathed river and going all the way to the bottom. Fortunately, it was not wide at that point, and despite my heavy boots and layers of thick clothing I managed to get to shore.

Soaked to the skin, I scrambled up the bank and cranked up a generator. I jumped the spark on a plug, got a fire started and rigged up a makeshift shelter with canvas. I huddled in it, hugging the fire while my clothes dried, shivering, miserable, but thoughtful.

I had gotten over my illness. Now, and for some time, I had been going downhill again. No job was worth that, and certainly this one was not.

It was time to pull out—to get completely out of the oil fields. My destiny wasn't here. I had never intended it to be. The West had been good to me, but it had done all it could. Now, it was my turn to do something, and something much better than what I had been doing.

My clothes dried. Dawn spread over the prairie. I kicked out the fire, walked into camp and quit.

# XXIX

I RETURNED TO Fort Worth in the winter of 1928. Except for the fact that Maxine had married, everything was about the same or more so. Pop was earning practically nothing. The family was barely skimping by.

I applied for a job at the hotel and was turned down flatly. The assistant managers and bell captains I had known were gone. The a.m. I applied to liked neither my appearance or my record.

"Nothing for you," he said curtly. "You've been in too much trouble around here. Anyway, you're too big to be hopping bells. A fellow as big as you ought to be out heaving coal."

"It doesn't have to be bell-hopping," I said, my face turning red. "I can hold almost any job around a hotel."

"Sorry."

"I'll tell you something," I said. "I think you're too little to be an assistant manager."

He grinned, coldly, and walked away.

I thought he had acted pretty ornery, but I couldn't greatly disagree with him on the point of my size. When I first went to work at the hotel, I had been well under six feet. Now, I was six feet four. While I was still underweight my broadened shoulders gave me the appearance of massiveness.

I was pretty self-conscious about my size. There were few other hotel jobs worth having, but I hadn't really wanted to hop bells. I was too big. Being a menial contrasted unpleasantly with the rugged independence of my recent years.

But I had to have a job, and quickly. So, unable to find anything else, I went to work in a chain grocery.

Theoretically, the work week was a mere seventy-four hours. Seven to seven on weekdays and seven to nine on Saturdays. The actuality, however, was something else. One had to arrive at six during the week to have the store ready for its seven o'clock opening, and at least another hour was spent in cleaning up and closing up at night. On Saturday, the biggest business day, one came to work at five and was lucky to get away in the early hours of Sunday morning. Sunday, or what remained of it, was usually spent at sales meetings, refurbishing the store or in taking inventory.

My salary was eighteen dollars a week.

I learned a very valuable lesson from this outfit, i.e., the longer the application blank, the worse the employer. This company insisted on knowing everything even remotely concerned with a prospective employee—everything from the size of his shoes to the religious and political preferences of his relatives. In fact, the only thing it was not interested in was how he could exist on a virtually nonexistent wage.

Although it was obviously a losing proposition, I held onto the job, looking around for another whenever I had the opportunity. This finally led me to a meeting with Allie

Ivers, who, since I knew what his attitude would be, I had hitherto avoided.

Allie had been permanently discharged from the hotel for dropping the baggage of a non-tipping guest out of a window. He was now the manager of a wildcat taxi service, a calling well suited to his superb gall and larcenous nature.

"You," he exclaimed, staring at me incredulously. "You are putting in a hundred hours a week for a lousy eighteen bucks? I'm ashamed of you, Jimmie! You can go back to the hotel."

"They won't take me," I said. "I'm too big."

"Keep on working in that store," said Allie, grimly, "and you won't be. They'll have you down in worse shape than you were before you went west. You can't feed yourself, let alone your family. You're about to be kicked out of your house and you all need clothes and medical attention. I'll tell you what's too big about you—your head. You think you're too good to hop bells."

"That's not it," I mumbled, although it was just about it. "Maybe I could have gone back, but I sort of told this assistant manager off."

"So what? You know how hotel men are. He probably laughed about it when he got off by himself. Anyway, there's two assistant managers and one sticks strictly out of the other's business."

"Well," I said, evasively, "how would I go about it?"

"How would you go about it," Allie mocked. "You stand there acting dumb and asking me. Get out of here! Get over there and get you a job."

I got out. I went over to the hotel.

I talked with the coffee shop manager and the maître d'. I talked with a room clerk, a couple of the auditors, the chief engineer and the steward. I knew all these people, and had done favors for them. They all agreed to put in a strong word in my behalf.

Now, an assistant manager is held responsible for anything that goes wrong on his shift, and a great many things can go wrong if his key personnel so choose. Insofar as his position will permit, he must be obliging with them.

It was Sunday afternoon when I talked with my various friends at the hotel. Having been unable to install a telephone at home, I waited around the lobby for the results.

The assistant manager on duty was the same one who had turned me down. He saw me and started toward me several times. Each time his phone rang, calling him back to his desk. After the last call, he motioned for me to come to him.

"Been studying you," he said, his mouth twitching. "You don't look nearly as big to me as you did."

"Yes, sir," I said. "You look a lot bigger to me."

He grinned good naturedly. "Well, like to come to work tonight?"

"Very much. If I can get a uniform altered to fit me."

"You will," he said firmly.

And I did.

Out of the great mass of stuff I had written in the oil fields, I had placed two short pieces with a locally published magazine of regional literature. The rate of pay had been low, but, because of its high standards, it was considered an honor to appear in it. I responded promptly when the editor, having learned that I was back in town, asked me to drop in for a visit.

I spent the larger part of an afternoon with him. He was a kindly man but a frank one, and I was able to accept his estimate of me without resentment. I had talent, he said, and also that dogged persistence without which talent was worthless. But that was just about all I had. Whatever my skill, I was writing from motives which were basically childish. I was trying to "get even" with people—to show 'em I wasn't so dumb as they thought I was, and to make them sorry for the many slights, real and fancied, which I had suffered. I lived too much inside myself. I needed to write more—much more—of what I saw, and less—much less—of what I wanted to see.

I was not well read, as I had thought myself. Here again I had tried to "show people," to prove that I knew more than they did. I had read something of everything but never everything of anything.

The editor thought it would help me immeasurably to go to college. College would bring some order to my chaotic efforts at self-improvement. It would help to bring me out of myself. I would be placed in an environment where writing was not looked upon as effete or slightly ridiculous.

He, himself, was an alumnus of the University of Nebraska. If I could see my way clear to enrolling, it was just possible that he could arrange a student loan for the tuition, or, perhaps, a small scholarship.

I thanked him and promised to think about it, but the project was obviously impossible. Financially speaking, we were just beginning to see daylight at home. And summer was coming on—always a bad time for hotel business.

I told Mom and Pop about it, and they insisted that I should go, by any and all means. Pop could find some way of maintaining himself. Mom and Freddie could stay with my grandparents who, as you will remember, lived in a small Nebraska town. But I just couldn't see it. All we had was each other, and I would be almost twenty-three years old when the fall school term started. It was crazy to think about it.

But, I did think about it, of course. And very unwisely I mentioned it to Allie.

"Hmmm," he mused. "I think you should go, Jimmie. How much dough would you have to have?"

"A lot more than I'll ever get," I said.

"Maybe not. I think I may be able to think of something."

I met him the following night, and he had indeed thought

of something. In fact, he had done a great deal more than think about it. I listened to his proposition, and told him flatly to go to hell.

"But what's wrong with it?" he inquired, putting on an air of great puzzlement. "There's big dough in it, and you don't have to invest any. What's wrong with selling whiskey?"

"It's against the law, for one thing!"

"So what? It won't be very long. Everyone knows prohibition's on the way out. Hell, you can clean up, Jimmie! You can get away with it where no one else could. You stand in good all over the hotel. The management trusts you, and—"

"They're going to keep right on trusting me, too!"

"You can wholesale—push the stuff with all the service employees. We'll see that they don't buy from anyone else, and you can hold the price up."

"Who's we?"

"Some of Al's boys. They're taking over here on the booze."

"Al? You mean—?"

"Uh-huh. That one. Incidentally, Jimmie, I don't think they'll like it if you turn this proposition down."

"They can lump it then," I scoffed. "Al Capone's boys! You mean Allie's, don't you? Get someone else to hustle your booze."

"It's not mine, honest." Allie held up a hand. "I'm not making a nickel on it. I was just trying to help you out."

"You'd better go back to stealing baggage," I said. "You're no good at lying any more."

I went on to work.

About one o'clock that morning, Mom called me. She sounded frightened.

"J-Jimmie. Two men—t-two men in a big Cadillac were j-just here."

"Yes?" I said. "What's the matter? What did they want, Mom?"

"I t-tried to stop them, but they came right on in. They left four cases of whiskey for you."

# XXX

**I** MET THEM the next morning, or, rather, they met me as I came out of the hotel's service entrance. Soft-spoken, modishly dressed young men, not a great deal older than I, they were not at all like the creatures which my study of gangster movies had led me to expect. We had breakfast together, and I felt encouraged to explain why I could not sell whiskey for them.

They listened quietly, without interruption. I finished my explanation, and still they sat waiting, staring at me steadily.

"Well"—I laughed nervously—"that's . . . you see how it is. I've never done anything like that, and—"

"What you going to do with the stuff, then?" one of them interrupted casually. "You can't sell it, what you going to do? How you going to pay for it?"

"Well, I—I—"

"You owe for four cases, ninety-eight a case. Call it three hundred and ninety dollars. You got the dough?"

"Look," I snapped, "I didn't order that stuff. You can come out to the house and pick it up, or I'll have it brought back to you. Any place you say. But—"

"You got the dough?" he repeated. "How you going to pay for it, then?"

"But I just finished telling— All right," I said. "All right. I'll sell this, but—"

"Good. You got a nice set-up there. Be good for ten, fifteen cases a week when you get organized."

It was like talking to a stone wall. They didn't argue. Their attitude was simply that there was nothing to argue about.

To be honest, I think I could have been firm at this point without serious danger to myself. I wasn't involved with them yet. They had too much to lose to risk trouble with someone who could appeal to the authorities with figuratively clean hands. They were paying off, of course, but no fix is ever solid. The purchaser is supposed to use it with discretion, to do nothing which will seriously embarrass the seller.

So, I had only to say no and keep saying it, and, I believe, the matter would have been ended. But despite a lifetime of pushing around, I had never developed a tolerance for it. And this latest instance, which had seriously frightened my mother, was particularly distasteful to me. It seemed to me that these characters needed to be taught a lesson, and that I was just the lad to do it.

"All right," I shrugged. "How much time do I have to pay up?"

"How much do you need?"

"Well, just getting started this way, it'll probably take me a week to sell it—all of it. Of course, I can pay you off a case at a time if—"

They didn't want to do that, as I was sure they would not. It would be too much trouble. Also, it bespoke a distrust which could be very unhealthy for the enterprise.

"We won't crowd you any. You have to run over a day or two sometime, why just say so. You play with us, we play with you. Later on, maybe, you can make it cash on the line."

"I couldn't do that for quite a while," I said. "Well, I could I guess, but—"

But they understood. I'd just been squeezing by. I and my family needed all sorts of things, and I was to go right ahead and take care of those needs. Naturally. That was as it should be. What was the sense in a guy working if he didn't have any dough to spend?

We'd wait awhile before going on a cash basis. Say, a couple of months from now.

We worked out the arrangements for delivery and payment. I went on home.

Pop was out of town for a few days, and was thus unaware of the previous night's happenings. Much against her will, I persuaded Mom to keep mum.

"I don't know why," she sighed. "I just don't know why it is you're always getting mixed up in something."

"I didn't mix up in it," I said. "I was mixed up."

"You certainly are! You're really mixed up if you think you can cheat those fellows. Honest to goodness, Jimmie, do you actually believe you can?"

"You wait and see," I promised. "I'll take those birds like Grant took Richmond."

The hotel was what was known in the trade as a "tight" or "clean" house. Bellboys returning from errands outside the hotel were always subjected to close scrutiny by the house detectives. If their uniforms bulged suspiciously, or if they were carrying a package of a certain size, they were almost certain to be searched. Whiskey was bootlegged, of course, in spite of all the hotel's precautions. But to carry out an operation of the size I contemplated was impossible by the usual pint-at-a-time methods. My base of operations, as I saw it, would have to be on the inside.

I have mentioned that a number of the lower-floor rooms were blocked off in hot weather. Since it was hot now, I purloined the key to one, using it as a storage room for whiskey which I brought in in inexpensive suitcases.

A supposed "guest" drove up at the side door and tapped his horn for a bellboy. I trotted out, removed his "baggage" and carried it up to my room. This same thing took place a dozen times a day with bona fide guests and baggage, so my comings and goings went unmarked, apparently, and while other boys had been caught and discharged and sometimes jailed for bringing in a pint, I brought in case after case. There was no trouble at all for quite a while.

I paid for the four cases promptly at the end of the week. The following week, having obtained a transfer to days, I sold six, and the week after that I sold seven. Each week I brought in a little more, paying up on the dot when the week was ended. In a very few weeks, I was handling and paying for upwards of ten cases.

Now, regardless of what my wholesalers thought, this was an enormous amount of whiskey to move in any hotel, even one that ran wide open. I had to re-wholesale of the bulk of it to other bellboys and service employees, taking a very short profit or no profit. And along toward the last, in order to get rid of the stuff, I sold several cases at a loss. On the overall transactions, of course, I made money—several times the sum I would have made at legitimate bell-hopping. But this was nothing like the amount which I might reasonably have been expected to make.

The money was spent almost as fast as I got it on clothes, on medical and dental attention, on a car which I had Mom buy and leave on the sales lot. These things and our day-to-day living expenses left me with very little surplus cash. "Al's boys" were scheduled to supply that—a quantity sufficient to travel on and to live on indefinitely and comfortably afterward.

The "boys" were just a little hesitant when, at the beginning of the week I meant to be my last, I ordered twenty cases. I had always paid off, hitherto, and I had an excellent reason for wanting so much, but still . . .

"This convention—you say it's going to be a big one?"

"You read the papers," I shrugged.

"How come you want all the stuff at once? Why don't you take part of it at the beginning of the week and part in the middle?"

"I always have got it all in at one time," I said.

"Yeah, but twenty cases. That's two grand."

"Well, let's let it go," I said, easily. "We'll have thirty-five bellboys working, and there's a chance I might be able to turn the whole twenty the first day or so. But give me five or ten or whatever you want to."

I got the twenty, but not without some uneasiness on the part of the boys. They hinted strongly that a substantial cash down payment would be welcome, and when I pleaded a shortage of money a partial pay-off for the mid-week was arranged.

That was fine with me. I wasn't going to be around by the middle of the week. If things went as I planned, I would work two days of the five-day convention and skip town.

I figured that I should at least be able to dump the whiskey at its wholesale price. Probably, with the house packed and so many boys working, I would do considerably better than that. With only a little luck, I should turn it for three thousand, or—if the breaks really fell my way—four or five thousand.

Anyway, it would be a very nice piece of change. Enough to give Pop a stake. Enough so that Mom and Freddie could live with me, when I entered the University of Nebraska, instead of staying with my grandparents.

The opening day of the convention was one of my long days—seven until noon, six until ten. As always, during the first shifts of a convention, there was very little fast money. The guests weren't limbered up yet. They were interested only in getting registered and cleaned up.

I sold two pints of whiskey at retail, and the remainder of a case—less one pint—at wholesale. That was every nickel I had in the world, a little more than a hundred dollars, when I knocked off at noon. I went home and to bed, intending to store up rest for the long hard grind I had ahead of me.

The whiskey would be reasonably safe from theft during these first two shifts, but it would not be safe after that. As soon as they got themselves orientated, and the booze market began to boom, every hot-shot bellboy in the hotel would be after the stuff. They would try to steal it from me, just as I was stealing it from my wholesalers. They would steal it, dump it and skip—exactly as I planned to do.

When I went back to the hotel tonight I would have to stay there—sleeping in the whiskey-storage room and never getting too far away from it—until I was ready to pull out. It would be tough, nerve-wracking. Almost thirty-six hours of staving off a three-sided peril. The wholesalers were suspicious of me and might become more than that at any minute. The hot-shots were out to rob me, the hotel detectives to catch me. The federal prohibition agents . . .

I had seen no signs of the prohibs so far, but that didn't mean they weren't on to me. Bushels of empty bottles were being carted out of the hotel every week. The management was getting alarmed. If the prohibition agents were on their toes at all . . .

It was too much to worry about. I closed my eyes and went to sleep.

About three that afternoon, Mom shook me awake.

"Jimmie! They found your whiskey. Prohibition officers!"

"Huh? What?" I sat up drowsily. "How do you know?"

"It just came over the radio. They got five cases, they said, and they're looking for the person it belongs to."

# XXXI

I WAS STILL half asleep, too drowsy for the moment to comprehend the true and terrible nature of my plight. As I recall it, I even laughed a little sleepily. Only five cases, huh? Well, that wasn't so bad. And as long as they didn't know who—

Then, it hit me, and suddenly I was wide awake and shivering. Five cases! Hell, if they had found five cases they had found it all! It had all been there in the one room. They'd only *reported* five cases, but they'd gotten every damned last bottle. Those prohibs—yes, and doubtless the assistant managers and house detectives—would be drinking my booze for the next six months.

They knew who the stuff belonged to all right. They'd just been waiting for me to get the cache built up good. Now, they'd knocked it over, and it was my cue to stay away from the hotel and keep my mouth shut. Otherwise—

But my wholesalers! I couldn't skip town now. I didn't have the money. And if I stayed here and couldn't pay them . . . ! For all I knew, they might have gotten the news already. They'd think I'd sold fifteen cases, and they'd want their dough. Probably, since I could no longer work at the hotel, they'd demand a settlement for the full amount. The loss of an alleged five cases to the prohibs would be my headache.

I pushed Mom out of the way and snatched up the telephone. I called Allie Ivers.

He had just heard the news himself, and his alarm was every bit as great as mine.

"I'm sorry as hell I got you into this, Jimmie. I just thought you could play it safe and easy, and—"

"I know, I know," I said. "I laid myself wide open. What had I better do?"

"Beat it. Get out of town as fast as you can."

"But I can't! I'll have less than a hundred bucks by the time I gas up the car. I've got a thousand miles to travel, and I have to take my mother and sister with me and—"

"You won't have a head left on your shoulders if you hang around here. I'm not kidding you, Jimmie. If I thought it was safe for you to wait until tomorrow I'd have you do it. I could scrape up some dough for you and—"

"Forget it," I said. "I'll-I guess we'll manage some way."

I hung up the telephone and began flinging on my clothes. I told Mom to start packing.

"Packing!" She stared at me incredulously. "*Packing!* Are you completely out of your—?"

"Don't pack, then. Just get ready to travel. Pop can take care of the other things later."

Mom grumbled, but she didn't argue much. Without understanding all the details, she knew I was taking the only way out of a very serious mess.

She called Freddie from the schoolgrounds where she was

playing with some other children. The two of them began to pack, and I called a taxicab.

I sped into town and got the car from the sales lot.

I had never seen it before, except from a distance. But Mom had always been a shrewd bargainer, and she seemed to have surpassed herself in this case. The body, the tires, the upholstery—all looked first-class. The motor seemed to be a little tight and sluggish, but that was only natural in a car which had been standing idle for several months.

Pop was at home when I returned. He was obviously displeased with the news of my bootlegging, but more concerned for my safety. I had to leave. The family was breaking up. It was no time for the reproaches which he must have felt like handing me.

We got the car loaded and made our farewells. Hardly more than an hour from the time of the radio news flash, Mom and Freddie and I were on our way out of town.

It was a scorching hot afternoon. We had gotten about five miles out on the highway when smoke began to rise from the hood. Before I could get to a filling station, some five miles farther, the motor was pounding ominously.

I got out and looked it over.

The radiator was full of water. The fan belt was okay, and the oil gauge stood at the full mark. I let the car cool awhile, then I drove on again.

The motor grew hotter, the pounding louder. Mom looked at me, frowning.

"What's the matter, Jimmie? Why does it do that?"

"We've got a flat crankshaft," I said. "It's been packed with sawdust and tractor oil. Now, it's working loose."

"Is it—will it cost much to fix?"

"It will. And it won't stay fixed. The bearings will work right loose again."

"But how . . . what in the world will we do?"

"Go as far as we can, then—well, we'll have to see when the time comes."

We rode on, and smoke and fumes poured up through the floor boards. The whole car shook with the pounding of the motor. Freddie stoppered her ears with her fingers and hung her head out the window. Mom snatched her back inside, turned on me furiously.

"Honest to goodness, Jimmie! What *is* the matter with you? This car's about to fall apart and we're practically broke and we've got to travel halfway across the United States and—and—and you sit there laughing! What's the matter with you, anyway? How can you do it?"

"I don't know," I said. "I guess I just don't know of anything else to do."